FRAMED

A Historical Novel about the Revolt of the Luddites

Christy Fearn

Published by Open Books 2013

Cover image "Loom of Fate" Copyright © John Novak

To learn more about the artist, visit http://johnnovak.net

ISBN: 061577153X

ISBN-13: 978-0615771533

For Greg

CONTENTS

PROLOGUE

'You must raise your right hand over your right eye. If there be another Luddite in company, he will raise his left hand over his left eye, like so,' the older man demonstrated. 'And then you must raise your forefinger of your right hand to the right side of your mouth; the other will raise the little finger of his left hand to the left side of his mouth.'

The younger man nodded.

'He will say, *what are you?* The answer, *determined.* And he will say, *what for?* Your answer?'

'Free Liberty!' the younger man said, smiling, his silver-blue eyes glinting in the dim light of the candle. The senior man took up a book that was lying on the table. He held it out.

'To seal your being twisted in, Mr Gordon, you must swear on the Bible. Repeat: I swear I will use my utmost endeavour to punish with death any traitor or traitors who rise against us, though he should fly to the verge of existence. So help me God to keep this oath inviolable.'

The young man held the Bible and repeated the oath.

1

'Now you must kiss the book.'

Mr Gordon lifted the book to his mouth and kissed it. He closed his eyes.

MARCH 1811

*L*izzie drew the curtains against the chill of the evening. She finished folding the pairs of stockings she had made. By the light of the candle she checked that they were all perfect; neat rows of stitches. She placed them in a basket next to her stocking frame and stretched her arms above her head. Her shoulders ached. St Mary's bells chimed six o'clock. Ten hours she had worked today. Robert would be home soon with their wages. There had been talk of another reduction. God knows how they would manage on any less.

She took up a knife and began peeling potatoes and parsnips for supper. She cut them into small pieces and placed them in a pot, added water and hung it over the fire. Looking up from the hearth, her eyes rested on her father's portrait. It was a miniature painting of him as a young man at about the same age as she was now. She wondered who had painted it and wished that she had asked him. Her rosary hung on a nail next to the portrait, in the space where her mother's picture had once been. Papa had taken that with him. Around the room were other empty shadows on the walls; ghosts of other pictures sold to buy food and firewood. Lizzie glanced at her stocking frame and remembered her father teaching her how to thread the needles. How difficult it had been to co-ordinate her small hands and feet which were barely able to reach the pedals. Her brother had always found it easier, despite his unwillingness to sit still. Such memories seemed like dreams when cast against the harsh realities of the present. What might the future bring?

Lizzie moved to the dresser, intending to fetch herbs for the stew; instead she opened one of the drawers. How long had it been since she had read her cards? She brought out the small wooden box, placed it on the table in front of her and slid open the lid. She removed the pack of decorated cards, shuffled them. She closed her eyes and cut the cards, then dealt them one at a time onto the table.

The first card was the Queen of Swords. The young woman depicted was frowning, holding the sword out in front of her in defense. Lizzie knew it meant that she would become involved in a conflict, a disagreement or an argument.

The recent past was represented by the Four of Wands. On the card, the wands were standing vertically on the ground, a garland of flowers around the top of them. Any happiness or celebration was behind her. Something was coming to an end.

What was the present problem? Lizzie turned over the next card. It was The Wheel of Fortune. *La Roue de Fortune*. Gold letters in ornate calligraphy above an image of a blindfolded woman turning the wheel. Unstoppable change. Something that would challenge and disturb.

The following card was *La Maison Dieu*. The House of God. Lizzie blinked. How could this be the solution to the problem? A tower was being struck by lightning; the card showed the building crumbling and falling. It meant taking radical action, destroying something longstanding.

Lizzie turned the penultimate card. The near future. It

was *Le Fou*. The picture showed a young person—Lizzie had never been able to tell if it was male or female—stepping off a cliff. The Fool did not look afraid. A little dog was apparently barking to warn the character, but The Fool was taking no notice. She would have to trust her instincts and be courageous.

The Knight of Cups was the final card. He would be someone Lizzie had yet to meet, in the far future. The youthful man on horseback was clad in silver armour and bore a large chalice rather than a weapon. He was someone who was passionate and idealistic.

Lizzie became aware that the stew was boiling rapidly, steam escaping from under the lid and wafting across the kitchen. She stirred the pot. The potatoes and parsnips were almost done. Their diet had been unchanged for over a month now. Occasionally augmented by beans or barley; it was becoming monotonous. She had discovered a patch of wild garlic growing near St Mary's last summer and she added the last of the dried bulbs to the stew. She replaced the lid and returned to the table, collected her cards and placed them back in the drawer.

Lizzie sat down to read the *Nottingham Journal*. General Napoleon was advancing and the English soldiers were on the march. She turned the pages. Further on there was a strange story about an undergraduate called Percy Bysshe Shelley, who had written a pamphlet called 'The Necessity Of Atheism.' It had apparently been on sale in a bookshop near Oxford University for only twenty minutes before being removed. She crossed herself.

The door opened. Robert entered the room and dropped his coat on a chair. His shoulders were hunched against the chill evening, his coal-black hair flopping over his forehead. Lizzie observed that tiny lines had appeared around his eyes; he would be displeased by that, having always been vain about his appearance. Ever since they were children he had been the one to spend the most time in front of the looking-glass. Lizzie would tease him, calling him '*Garçon jolie*'. A little shorter than average in height, at least he was unbowed by working at a frame every day. His faded linen shirt hung loosely around his chest. The collar and cuffs were beginning to fray. Robert usually had money for ale; nowadays rarely for clothes. His arms still looked strong, although his cheeks were as hollow as hers. He shook a handful of coins from his purse onto the table. '*Il fait mauvais*,' he said. His voice was resigned and hinted at apology.

Lizzie surveyed the amount. 'Is that really all there is?' She shook her head in disbelief.

'That's both yours and mine.'

'Both?! Are you sure?' Lizzie's eyes met Robert's. 'Or have you been to the Angel on your way home? Did you lose at cards again?'

'I'm not a child.' Robert's expression was surly.

'One of us has to be the *responsible*,' Lizzie snapped.

Robert grimaced. 'You're only two minutes older than me; I'll do what I want with my money.'

'When you gamble away your earnings, we both lose.' She could not believe he had been so stupid. 'How much did you lose?'

Robert was silent. He had not intended to lose, but neither could he see the point in saving.

'How much?!'

Robert looked up from under his dark brow. She could read his expression; it was the mirror of her own.

'*La totalité*?! All of it?!'

Robert watched as Lizzie scooped up the coins. She placed them in a drawer of the dresser and locked it. Then she put the key in her pocket. 'You are not going to lose mine as well.' Then she took the pot from the fire and began to ladle the stew into bowls.

'I wouldn't do that,' Robert said.

'How can I be sure?' She passed a bowl to him.

Robert began to eat, his stomach growling with hunger.

He tried to eat more slowly in order to make it last. Steadily their meals were becoming more meagre as the money appeared to be worth less every day. Bread was simply unaffordable. Prices rose, but wages did not. Why should a man be unable to afford to feed himself properly? Why should he not be able to have a game of cards now and again? Yet Robert was grateful that she was able to make a decent dinner from a few vegetables. He looked up at Lizzie. 'I'm sorry.' His dark eyes were like those of a deer.

Lizzie's heart softened a little. He was still her *jumeau*, her mirror image. She would always have to look after him. She remembered how she had warned him about climbing into the trees in the churchyard to collect chestnuts; he had fallen, of course, but made her swear not to tell Papa. Lizzie wondered why Robert felt the need to take risks all the time. He was also careless in his choice of friends. Her stew was too hot for her to eat so she blew across it. 'All right,' she said, 'but you will please promise me that you will not gamble anymore. Especially with Ben Harwood; I don't trust him.'

'Ben's a good friend,' Robert retorted. 'If it wasn't for him, we'd have even less.'

'How is that?'

'He's asked his uncle to keep us on. They're getting rid of stockingers left, right and centre.'

Lizzie did not like the idea of being beholden to Ben or to Mr Betts. 'Our work is good enough to speak for itself, surely?' she said.

Robert shook his head. 'No, only tonight when I went to collect the wages, the factor said they're replacing half of us with colts.'

Lizzie almost dropped her spoon. 'But they're untrained! They don't know how to do anything!'

'I know. But that doesn't matter. Betts isn't bothered about quality any more. All he's interested in is quantity. Profit and speed.'

'Ridiculous,' Lizzie hissed. 'So what'll happen now?'

'Well, as you're paid less, they'll probably keep you on. I might be out of a job by the end of the year.' Robert wiped his bowl with a crust of bread, and sat back in his chair. 'That was delicious, by the way,' he said. Lizzie rubbed her brow.

'They're replacing some of the frames at the workshop as well,' Robert said.

'What about Papa's?' She glanced over at the frame she had worked every day since he'd gone.

'You'll be keeping that for the moment. I think even Betts knows that your silk stockings will make him a decent return. He's on about exporting the best stuff.'

'What are they replacing the other frames with?'

'Larger gauge.'

'So they can make more for fewer wage,' Lizzie sighed.

Robert nodded. 'And if we object, they'll just get rid of us,' he added.

Lizzie finished her stew. 'We must be able to do something.'

'Well, some of the men are having a meeting. I'm going. I see no reason why you can't go along as well.' Robert paused. 'Although, I think they might be planning something more than just talking.'

Lizzie frowned. 'What do you mean?'

Robert's expression was devious. 'Getting rid of what's threatening our jobs.'

'*Sabotage*?' Lizzie's eyes were saucers.

'In a manner of speaking.'

'Do you think you could get away with it?'

'As long as it was under cover of night and unidentified, I think so.'

Lizzie considered what he was saying. 'But it would only be the frames that would put us out of work?'

'Yes. Just the ones in the workshops. We'll dismantle them, stop them being used for cut-ups.'

'And I just carry on as before? Pretend I know nothing

about it?'

'You must,' Robert asserted. 'After all, one of us has to be the *responsible* one.' He smiled.

'You will be careful, though,' Lizzie said. 'You are still my little brother.'

'Only by two minutes,' he laughed. He took her hand. 'Of course I'll be careful. And I promise I won't gamble any more.'

APRIL 1811

On the fourth stroke of the hammer the door gave way. Men poured into the room and set about the machines with their improvised weapons. An axe more regularly used for chopping firewood shattered the needle sinkers on the first frame. The next succumbed to blows from a poker. Splinters of wood flew out, bobbins unravelled and rolled along the floor.

One of the men tore half-finished stockings from the frames and ripped them into threads. He then laid into the frame with the hammer. Looking around him, he laughed, 'They look like kindling now.'

Robert abandoned guarding the door and hurried in: 'Someone's coming,' he hissed. 'It sounds like there's a lot of them.'

'If they get in our way, Robert, I'll break their bones like we've broke the frames!' smirked the man who had destroyed the stockings.

From around the corner, a group of men appeared. 'It's the militia!' cried Robert. 'Everybody out! Scatter and they'll not catch us.'

They pulled their kerchiefs up over their noses and fled. Two men disappeared down Short Hill, through Trivett Square and were gone, off towards the river. Another dashed up Weekday Cross, turned sharply left down to Broadmarsh. Robert, aware of the sound his footsteps were making rushed headlong up Stoney Street, the soldiers gaining on him. He concealed himself in a passageway near the church.

His heart pounded, he could feel his blood thumping through him, his breath steam in the chill air. Leaning against the cold wall, he closed his eyes.

'One of them went down here!' he heard a man shout.

Immediately he realised he had nowhere to go. Still panting, he looked at the church. 'Hail Mary, full of Grace,' he whispered. Then he grasped the railings and heaved himself up. Carefully placing his hands between the points, he launched himself over. He landed on soft grass and lay motionless among the daffodils in the dank graveyard.

'He's not here,' he heard one of them say.

'He must have gone up towards Hockley,' said another.

Gradually their voices faded and he was alone. He rolled over onto his back, stared at the stars and sighed with relief. 'Thank you, Our Lady,' he whispered.

MAY 1811

'Robert, how long are you going to be?'

Lizzie swept the breakfast breadcrumbs off the table, collecting them in her apron. She shook them out the door. Immediately sparrows swooped down to make the most of the free food. Robert scraped the last of the soap from his chin. A tiny ruby of blood grew and fell into the water. It bloomed into swirling petals. He winced, dropping the razor, and snatched up a towel. He patted his face and hoped the nick would not show. He brought the bowl through the kitchen, out to the street, and tipped the now pink water into the gutter. Lizzie was leaning against the wall, the dawn sun warming her face. The street was silent. Robert stopped in front of her.

'How do I look?'

Lizzie opened her eyes. She smiled. '*Très beau.*' She followed him back inside. 'Who are you hoping to impress?' she asked.

Robert blushed. 'Is it so obvious?'

'You're easy to read.' She picked up her shawl. 'I'm not sure I'll need this, it's so warm already.'

Robert pulled on his jacket, and after checking that his neck wasn't bleeding, tied his neckerchief. He lingered in front of the mirror, sweeping his hair with his hands. Forwards, backwards, he was not content. How he wished he could afford a barber. Robert frowned. There would be girls at the fair. One in particular he hoped to see.

'Do you think you should cut my hair before we go?'

Lizzie stood next to him, their faces parallel in the glass. She placed her hands on his shoulders. 'There isn't time,' she said. 'You're vain; worse than a girl. I don't look at myself half as much!' She gave him a playful jab in the ribs.

'Gah! That hurt!' He spun round to grab her but she was too swift. Robert laughed as he chased her around the table. They dodged each other until eventually he caught her and they both erupted in childlike giggles.

'Papa would say that we've never grown up,' Robert gasped.

Lizzie turned towards him and ran her fingers through his hair. 'Now don't touch it,' she ordered, 'it looks perfect.'

Robert looked into the mirror once more. He turned his head from side to side. Lizzie had arranged his hair so that it swept from one side to the other. 'Do I look like one of the *Incroyables*?' he asked.

'I think the fashionable men call themselves *dandy* now.'

'Dandy? What, like a turkey?!'

Lizzie chuckled. 'That's what they say.'

'And I suppose I should strut like a cock?' Robert flapped his elbows and clucked.

Lizzie laughed as she picked up her shawl. 'Come on Mr Turkey, let's go. 'Maybe I'll sell you at the fair,' she teased.

He followed her out of the house and down the road, still squawking and gobbling. The more he flapped his arms, the more she laughed.

The street was unusually quiet. As on a Sunday, many

of the workers were still in bed; the one day they did not have to be up before dawn. As the twins moved through the cobbled streets, they dodged the stream of sewage that slid along the gutter like a rivulet of foul treacle. The chimneys, which would normally be belching smoke, were inactive. Most of the begrimed cottages that crowded around the communal water pump were in desperate need of repair, the ragged lace curtains in the windows being the only testament that anyone lived within.

Lizzie caught Robert's hand and they began to dance a childish ballet. As they turned the corner, they immediately collided with Père Bertrand, who was on his way to the chapel. His robes flapped and billowed as he flung his arms out to regain his balance, but failed to do so. Both helped the floundering priest to his feet.

'*Mes enfants*! What on earth were you doing?' He dusted himself off ineffectually as Robert began to explain.

'You see, I was pretending to be a turkey cock.'

Both he and Lizzie attempted to stifle giggles. Père Bertrand peered at them over his spectacles, shaking his head.

'It is surely some sort of May Day madness, imitating *les oiseaux*. Whatever next?'

'Forgive our high spirits,' Lizzie ventured, picking up his prayer book. 'We don't work today. And there is a fair!'

'Ah,' Bertrand nodded, 'I see. So you make Matins in the style of birds,' he sighed. 'I expect to see you both at Mass.' He looked from one to the other.

'Yes, Father.' Both Robert and Lizzie looked suitably chastened.

'Well, off you go. Enjoy your *jour en conge. Au revoir.*'

He began to make his way up the street. They watched him for a moment, then linked arms and ran down the hill.

When Lizzie and Robert arrived in Sneinton the stalls were already set out, traders plying every kind of food and trinket. Sweets and pastries glowed golden in the sun;

grains of sugar glittered on the surface. There were lace tablecloths and collars, shawls and handkerchiefs on display. A rotund gentleman with a nose like a strawberry called out: 'Hot cakes! Pastries and buns! Only a penny!' As they passed between the stalls they came across a small crowd of people watching a man stripped to the waist, his muscles like knotted iron, holding a sword aloft. The woman next to him held out her arms to one side to draw attention to him. 'Watch the amazing Mr Steel, as he attempts this death defying feat!' Lizzie and Robert stood motionless as the man dropped his head backwards and opened his mouth. Lizzie covered her eyes and the crowd gasped as Mr Steel lowered the blade into his mouth. He proceeded to slide the sword down his throat until it was almost to the hilt. Robert grinned and applauded. He nudged Lizzie. 'I can't look' she said.

The woman moved to the other side as Mr Steel held his arms out, the sword balanced inside his chest. After a few seconds he slowly withdrew it. Brandishing the blade, he bowed.

He noticed Lizzie with her eyes shut tight. He strode over to her: 'Do not fear, Miss,' he boomed, 'there is no harm done!' The crowd applauded and cheered, and Lizzie giggled with relief. Mr Steel patted her on the shoulder and moved away to meet his admirers. Robert took her hand. 'I hear music!' he said.

From one corner a tinkling hurdy-gurdy provided the accompaniment to a group of small children that were dancing in imitation of their elders. The little boys executed bows to the girls' curtsies as they performed their miniature gavotte. Brightly coloured ribbons fluttered in the breeze at the haberdasher's stall and the aroma of cheese, bread and bacon wafted through the air. Lizzie and Robert wandered through the market, becoming part of the increasing throng.

At one end they reached the maypole, a circlet of flowers resting on the top. The long tapes were outstretched, held by boys and girls little younger than themselves. A handful of musicians began to play, an animated, bearded fiddler leading them, beating time with his foot. As the youths wove in and out, their ribbons began to lattice around the pole. The girls skipped between them, twirling as they danced. When they finally came to rest, the crown of blossom had slid from the top of the pole to the bottom. The bashful boys kissed the girls very chastely on the cheek and then bowed. The crowd applauded and the fiddler, piper and drummer struck up again.

Robert heard the cake seller calling out once more. 'I'm hungry again, now,' he said.

'You're always hungry,' said Lizzie.

'Would you like some cake?' He pulled out a couple of coins.

'Alright then.'

Lizzie arranged her shawl on the ground and sat down, and Robert approached the cake stall. While he was gone she watched a group of men on the other side of the maypole that were wearing red coats and standing close to a tent-like canvas canopy. They were laughing loudly, slapping each other on the back. Lizzie held her hand above her eyes to shield her view from the sun. A very smart looking man in a similar red coat but with a glinting gold braid decorating his shoulders rode up. He dismounted and walked over to them. Instantly their behaviour changed. They saluted him. He was obviously important. Although he motioned to them to be at ease, they still looked slightly nervous. After having a few words with one of the officers, he climbed back on his horse and rode away.

Robert returned with the cakes. 'Here you are. It's the same man that sells gingerbread at Christmas. I recognise him.' He settled down to eat. He noticed that Lizzie was preoccupied. Munching his cake, he followed her gaze. 'Oh aye, the army's still here. Making sure we behave ourselves,' he grimaced. 'You would've thought they'd be too busy chasing Bonaparte to be in Notts getting drunk and chasing girls.'

Just as Robert spoke, a rather striking young woman walked past the soldiers and they roared their approval. Robert jumped to his feet. 'Sarah!' he shouted, but the girl was too far away to hear him. 'Wait here,' he said to Lizzie as he ran toward her. Lizzie watched as he approached her; he took Sarah's hand and kissed it gallantly. Some of the soldiers jeered, turned away and resumed drinking; others began to look for alternative prey.

As Robert talked with Sarah, a tall young man approached them from the opposite direction. He walked up behind Sarah and, in a rather forward fashion, put his hands over her eyes. She clearly knew who he was, because she turned to him and gave him a playful slap. As she did so, he held her tightly round the waist and gave her a brazen kiss. Robert looked away and rubbed his chin, something he always did when he felt put out. When the couple had finished kissing, he led them over to Lizzie. She stood up.

'Lizzie, you remember Ben Harwood, from the workshop?'

Ben lifted Lizzie's hand and kissed it. His golden hair glowed in the sun. 'You're pretty as ever,' he smiled.

'And this is Sarah.' Robert blushed as he said her name. Lizzie shook her hand.

'Heavens, you're the dead spit of each other!' Sarah grinned. Ben slipped his arm around Sarah's waist.

'Why don't we get some beer?' he suggested.

Sarah smiled. 'The landlady from The Angel has a stall here. One of the soldiers is cagged, so he said I could have his share.'

'What do you mean?' asked Robert.

'He's vowed not to drink, so there are five bumpers going begging,' laughed Ben.

'*Allons-y!*' said Robert, which sent Sarah into fits of

giggles.

With that they began to walk in the direction of the stall. Sarah indicated some tables with benches beside them.

'You sit down; I'll get the drinks.'

Emma unscrewed the tap on the end of the barrel and began to fill the pint pots.

'I'm not going to make a profit if you keep blagging from the bloodcoats.'

'Don't worry,' Sarah reassured her, 'I'm sure this won't be the only round. We'll pay for the next lot.'

She picked up two of the beers and ferried them over to Ben and Robert. 'There you are, gentlemen. Plenty more where they come from.' She returned to the stall.

'I'll make sure you get enough business the rest of the week as well.' Sarah winked at Emma.

'You've got the cheek of the devil,' the landlady smiled as she handed over the three pints. She placed them on a tray for Sarah.

'They've just been paid,' Sarah nodded towards the soldiers, 'and they're eager to spend when they're flush. I'll make sure they do that at The Angel.'

Sarah sat down next to Ben. 'Where's Lizzie?'

'She's gone to buy some ribbons.' Robert glanced over at the stall.

'They're so pretty! I must go and have a look.' Sarah took a sip of her beer then got up. 'Don't wait for me, you get it down you.'

Robert laughed as he watched her hurry over to Lizzie. Ben gulped his beer. He wiped his mouth with the back of his hand.

'She's a fubsey wench, isn't she?' he grinned.

'She's lovely,' Robert replied without thinking. He clumsily corrected himself. 'Comely, I mean. Yes, fubsey.'

'You've got the hots for her, admit it.' Ben whispered. Then he burst out laughing. 'I'm going to take a flyer again with her later.'

'Does that mean—' Robert began.

'I've had her once already today,' Ben bragged. 'She's got no shame. She'll do it anywhere.'

Robert gazed at Sarah. She and Lizzie were comparing lengths of lace and silk. Sarah's auburn hair was glowing in the sunshine. Her revealing decolletage a marked contrast to Lizzie's modest dress. He tried to push the thought of Sarah and Ben from his mind, but found he could not. He imagined himself with her instead. At that very moment Sarah turned round to face him. She waved and then began to tie the ivy green ribbon in her hair. Lizzie helped her to secure it.

Ben was half way through a second pint; he nudged Robert. 'Catch up, Bob! I'll fetch some more.' He looked over at the girls. 'Your sister's very fine, very proud.'

Robert resumed drinking. 'She is that.'

'I reckon any man that married her would be hen-pecked. Does she boss you about?'

'A bit,' Robert admitted. 'She knows her own mind. She's very responsible.'

Ben grinned. 'What she needs is a good—'

Robert cut in: 'What?'

'A good *man*... To tell her what's what.' Ben downed his ale.

'I'd like to see anyone try,' Robert chuckled.

Ben indicated the empty pint pots to Sarah and Lizzie when they returned.

'You best drink up, ladies.' He counted out coins. 'I'll get us some more in a moment.' He wandered over to the beer stall. Sarah picked up her beer and began to drink, absent mindedly twirling one of her russet curls as she did so. Lizzie realised that Robert was enamored with her.

'Do you like my ribbons?' Sarah turned her head so Robert could see.

'*Très jolie*,' he said. He wanted to say she was '*baisable*', he wanted to have her, as Ben had had her.

'What does that mean?' Sarah turned to face him, her hazel eyes shining. 'Is it French?'

Robert nodded, 'It means *very pretty*,' he murmured.

Lizzie was willing him to kiss Sarah. Maybe if they were alone Robert would be more courageous. She stood up. 'I'll help Ben with the drinks.'

When Lizzie had walked a few yards, she turned back to look at them. Robert took Sarah's hand and kissed it. He leaned a little closer to her. Sarah placed her firm hands on Robert's shoulders, drew him towards her and began to kiss him.

'I hope he's paid for that.' Lizzie turned to face Ben as he handed her two tankards of beer.

'Take them over, and tell Robert not to wear her out,' he smirked, 'I'll bring the other two pints.'

Lizzie took the tankards and froze for a moment. She looked back at Robert and Sarah. It didn't seem as though Sarah needed the promise of payment to kiss him. Was Ben serious? A pretty girl like Sarah would attract suitors with her looks, but, selling her body? Lizzie approached them and sat down once more. Robert's dark eyes were bright with excitement as he took the drinks from her.

'*Merci*,' he said, and passed Sarah one of the pints.

'I'd better move out of the sun.' Sarah swapped seats with Lizzie so that she was opposite Robert rather than next to him. 'I don't want to get a red face,' she said, then added, 'you don't need to worry, being so dark.' Sarah stroked Robert's cheek.

Ben returned with the remaining drinks. Straddling the bench, he settled himself next to Sarah and slurped his beer. Lizzie watched as Ben took Sarah's hand and squeezed it. 'Do you want to see me make a few florins from the redcoats?' He nodded towards the soldiers; some of them were gambling with cards.

'Fancy your chances, do you?' Sarah gave Ben a saucy look.

Lizzie noticed that Sarah was scratching Ben's arm,

leaving red streaks on his pale skin. He smiled; clearly he was enjoying it.

'It'd mean I'd have more to spend later,' he grinned. Sarah bit her lip and giggled.

'Why don't we both challenge them?' Robert placed his empty tankard firmly on the table. 'We'll split the winnings.'

Lizzie shot Robert a warning look, but he ignored it.

'You're on!' Ben finished his pint and stood up. 'Coming with us, ladies?' He placed his hands on Lizzie's shoulders. Instinctively she flinched.

'Don't be afraid Lizzie,' he said, smiling. 'We'll empty their pockets, won't we Rob?'

'I'll introduce you,' said Sarah. 'I've already spoken to a couple of them.'

One of the two young soldiers stood up as they arrived at the card table. 'She's back again, the angel!'

'Tom, isn't it? These two gentlemen are Ben and Robert, and they've come to challenge you.'

Tom put his hand out to Ben. 'Private Tom Greenway. Fancy your chances, do you?'

'That's just what I said,' giggled Sarah.

Lizzie rubbed her brow. She tried to take hold of Robert's elbow. She wanted to lead him to safety, but he shook her hand away. The second soldier noticed and took Lizzie's hand himself.

'Don't you worry about him. Come and sit by me, my dark charmer. You can bring me luck.'

Lizzie allowed him to guide her to his chair. He gave a formal bow.

'Private Callum McRae. And who are you, my bonny lass?'

'Lizzie Miller,' she said, exchanging a look with Robert, praying that he would play along with the pseudonym.

Robert nodded. 'She's my sister,' he said.

McRae unfolded a field seat for himself, laughing as he

did so. 'I never would have guessed. You're like two wee peas.' He shuffled and began to deal the cards. 'Tam, does she not remind you of that lady in Lisbon?'

Greenway puffed on his pipe. He cocked his head to one side. 'Which one?' he asked.

'All of them.' McRae chuckled.

Ben sat and reached behind him. Lizzie saw him stroke Sarah's hand. Sarah grasped his elbow. From where Sarah was sitting, she was able to see both Ben's and Greenway's cards. Judging by his expression, Robert's cards were not fortunate. Ben's face, however, gave nothing away.

'Place your bet.' Greenway dropped several coins in the middle of the table. The others matched his wager. Robert's eyes gleamed as he added his coins plus two extra ones.

McRae raised his eyebrows. 'Your brother's feeling flush.'

They each took a card from the pile and discarded one of the originals. Lizzie sighed. With each round, Sarah subtly squeezed Ben's elbow, once to agree with him, twice to disagree, so that he knew which cards to drop and which to keep. The stack of coins grew. The canvas canopy flapped in the breeze and the clouds gathered. Eventually Ben called a halt, raising his hand. He arranged his cards on the table, fanning them out slowly. McRae slapped his thigh and showed his own hand. Originally, he had been collecting Aces and Jacks himself.

'Will you look at that? He had four bullets and three knaves, would you credit it?'

Greenway shook his head. He knocked the spent tobacco from his pipe and set about refilling it.

'You bastard!' he grinned.

Ben scooped up all the coins. Robert dropped his cards on the table and watched Ben give Sarah four shillings.

'Shall I fetch us some drinks?' she asked.

'Not for me,' said Greenway, 'I'm on the wagon for six weeks.'

'I'll not say no,' McRae smiled.

Ben and Sarah held hands as they disappeared to the ale stall. Lizzie watched Robert as he failed to hide his disappointment. McRae turned to him.

'Hey, laddie, don't be downhearted.' He patted Robert on the back. 'At least you've got your health and your pretty sister to console you.'

Lizzie felt his bristly chin as he pecked her on the cheek. She shivered a little in the cool breeze. McRae helped her lift her shawl onto her shoulders. His kind eyes were the colour of gun-metal.

'How would you like to stay with me, m'dear? It may be my last night here.' He gently kissed her hand. There was a heavy rumble of thunder. Suddenly, in her mind's eye Lizzie could see McRae, surrounded by smoke, lying in what looked like a barn; his face death-pale, a gunshot wound in his shoulder. She blinked and met Robert's gaze. McRae noticed their eerie silence. He clicked his fingers.

'Hey, you two look as though you've seen a sprite.'

Lizzie turned to him. A sudden flash of lightning lit up the young soldier's face. Robert stood up. 'Let's go,' he beckoned to Lizzie.

Lizzie kissed McRae's forehead. Then she stood. 'Adieu,' she said.

McRae was dumbfounded. The rain began to beat a retreat on the canopy.

'What was the meaning of that?' asked Greenway.

McRae scratched his head. 'Lord knows, though I doubt I'll be seeing her again.'

Robert removed his jacket and held it aloft so that they could both shelter under it. They ran towards town, pausing for sanctuary in a doorway.

'Did you see his future?' asked Robert. The heavy raindrops began to blacken the pavement. Lizzie nodded. 'He was dead. He'd been shot.' She was unsure whether her face was wet with rain or tears.

Robert leaned against the door. 'God, I can't believe I lost all that money,' he groaned.

Lizzie wedged herself in beside him. 'Ben agreed to give you half the winnings; at least you haven't lost your life.'

'He'll probably spend it all on Sarah.' His voice was almost a sob.

'Do you really think so? Is she a *putain*?'

Robert looked down at the ground, rivulets of muddy water dribbling down the street, but he didn't answer.

'Is she?' Lizzie asked. The sky crackled with lightning.

'I don't know...' He turned to Lizzie. 'Yes, she is. But I love her!'

The relentless rain clattered around them. Lizzie took Robert's hand. She shouted above the storm. 'Why don't you tell her?'

'She's too warm for Ben. He's a better prospect. He stands to inherit. What can I offer her?' He looked dejected, his dark hair dripping in glossy waves.

'Your honesty. Your love.'

They remained in the doorway as the rods of rain encaged them. They were silent for a moment, smelling the wet pavement and the sodden wool of Lizzie's shawl. Eventually the rain began to ease off.

Lizzie took Robert's arm. 'Let's make a run for it,' she said, 'I don't think it's going to stop.'

Robert held his jacket above them once again as they splashed their way towards Barker Gate.

JUNE 1811

'Will you be coming to Ashfield with us tomorrow?'

Ben sighed. 'If you like, Mother.'

Katherine Harwood looked up from her needlepoint. 'I would like it. You know your father's side of the family sees you so rarely.' She rested the small wooden embroidery frame on her knee. 'Besides, your aunt always gives us a generous Sunday luncheon.' She glanced at her son.

'Alright, you've whet my appetite.' Ben walked over to his mother and kissed her cheek, 'I'm starving now, as it happens.'

'If you can't wait until your uncle's ridden back from Arnold, why don't you go to the kitchen and ask Annie to make you some supper?'

Katherine patted Ben's hand. He nodded and left her to her sewing.

Annie kneaded the dough. The sunshine glowed on her hair, turning it the pale colour of ripe corn. Concentrating on the rhythmic movements, she was unaware of the visitor to the kitchen.

'I'm hungry.' Ben leant against the door, closing it behind him.

Annie looked up. 'Master Harwood! You made me jump.' She wiped her hands on her apron as Ben strode over to her.

'What are you making?'

'Jam tarts.'

Ben's nose wrinkled, 'Too sweet for me. I want something savoury.' He stood very close to her. Annie looked uncomfortable. She turned to the larder.

'I could toast you some pikelets, or muffins.'

Ben stepped towards her once more. He towered over her. 'How old are you now, Annie?'

An unexpected question: the maid took a nervous step backwards. 'Sixteen, sir.' Ben rested his elbow on a shelf, preventing her from leaving the larder.

'So you've been here a year.'

Annie nodded.

'It's strange, until now I'd not noticed how much you'd grown. You were a little girl.'

Annie blushed.

'But now...' Ben reached forward and pulled the flimsy muslin shawl from Annie's shoulders. It revealed her neck and collarbone. Ben tugged the corners of the shawl from inside the front of Annie's bodice. He stared at her breasts.

'If I don't get the pastry rolled out,' Annie blurted, 'the tarts won't be ready in time for supper,'

Ben sniggered. 'Fuck the pastry.'

Annie gasped.

'You've never heard such words, have you?' Ben sneered. 'Do you even know what it means?'

Annie shook her head, but her red cheeks betrayed her.

'It's something very wicked.' Ben took hold of her wrists and pulled her towards him. Then he moved her backwards to the kitchen table and easily lifted her onto it.

'No, Master Harwood. Please don't hurt me. I've done

nothing wrong.' She was rigid with fear. 'I'll do anything you ask, but please do not hurt me.'

'I'm not going to hurt you, you silly girl.' He forced her knees apart with his own and pressed her mouth with a rough kiss.

'What are you going to do?' Annie's voice was a whisper.

'Now that you're a fully grown woman, I'm going to fuck you.'

'No!' she cried.

She struggled but Ben's strength was overpowering. He pushed her skirts up and unbuttoned his breeches. Annie managed to extract one of her hands and she strained to take hold of the rolling pin, but it was out of her reach. Her fingertips nudged it and it clattered onto the stone floor. Unable to find a weapon, she slapped Ben hard across the face.

'You shouldn't have done that,' he snarled. 'It makes me want you even more.'

'Stop!' she screamed, her cry turning into a sob as he entered her.

The kitchen door flew open.

'What in God's name do you think you're doing?!'

Matthew Betts stormed into the kitchen. He seized his nephew by the scruff of the neck and tore him away from Annie. She climbed off the table and straightened her skirts, wiping tears from her eyes with her apron.

'Wait in my study!' Mr Betts ordered her. Annie, shaking, curtseyed and hurried out of the kitchen. She closed the door behind her.

Mr Betts slammed Ben against the wall, his face parallel to his nephew's.

'How dare you? How dare you show such a lack of restraint? You have no morals. No self-control. It's as though the Devil himself were inside you.'

Ben gasped for breath.

'You're consumed with lust. I'm going to beat it out of you.' Mr Betts brandished his horsewhip. He dragged Ben away from the wall and pushed him face down onto the table. He began to lash Ben's back with the riding crop.

'It wasn't my fault!' Ben shouted. 'That bitch was flaunting herself at me.'

'You will be silent!' Betts continued to beat his nephew. Ben cried out with every stroke. Finally the older man hauled Ben upright and pinned him to the wall once more. The lashes on Ben's back stinging, he was silenced by the pain.

'There will be no word of this to your mother. I shall see that Annie is suitably reprimanded. But if I find you two together again, my wrath will be terrible. Do I make myself clear?'

Ben nodded, unable to speak.

'Do I make myself clear?' Mr Betts hissed.

Ben croaked his reply, 'Yes, uncle.'

'Can we sacrifice one of our sheets?' Robert called from the bedroom. 'What should we use for the letters? Blacking?'

Lizzie considered for a moment. 'We could sew them, with pieces of waste cloth. The words might be clearer.'

Robert brought a sheet to the kitchen. He spread it out over the table.

'It's too big. Let's cut it lengthways, then a few of us can hold it in front.' He took a pair of shears, slit the sheet and tore it in half. Lizzie took one end and they laid it on the floor.

'This isn't how you usually spend Saturday night, is it?' She looked at Robert. He shook his head. Lizzie fetched the basket of discarded cloth. 'I'm glad you're not out gambling or drinking.'

Robert's face was serious. 'This is more worthwhile,' he said, drawing a deep breath. 'What's it to be then, *God protect the trade*?'

'No,' Lizzie decided, 'I can think of something that will be easier to sew in capitals.'

She found pieces of dark fabric and arranged letters on the sheet to spell out the slogan. Pinning them to the cloth, the twins took needles and thread and began to sew them from one side to the other. **G I V E   U S   B R E A D!**

Once they had finished, they stepped away to admire their work. 'It's to the point,' she stated. Robert agreed.

'Rain before seven, fine before eleven. I've never believed that. How can it be? It can't be the same weather every time, can it?' Robert munched his porridge as a shower spattered against the window.

'I suppose not,' Lizzie said as she sliced the last of the loaf. She had to saw at it; the stale crust resisted the knife.

'Is there any cheese?' Robert asked with a look of doubt in his eyes.

'A tiny bit... I'll cut it fine so we can both have some.'

Lizzie placed the wafer thin slices of cheese between the bread, wrapped them in a cloth and tied string around the parcel. 'At least we'll have something to eat this afternoon,' she told him. 'Only parsnips left for supper.'

Robert groaned, 'Not again.'

'It's all we can afford,' Lizzie sighed.

'Is there no more garlic?'

'I had a look around in the churchyard, but all I could find was nettles.'

Robert grimaced: 'I keep dreaming about cakes and pastries, roast duck and green beans.' He leaned on his hands, resting his palms on his forehead. 'How is it fair? We work all the hours God sends and we have to survive on crusts and roots. It's like we're being punished for being alive.'

Lizzie sat next to him. She stroked his hair.

'That's what today is about. We shall make sure we are heard,' she sighed. 'Although, it'll mean missing Mass.'

Robert took Lizzie's hand. 'This is more important,' he

said. '*Fraternité*!'

'*Fraternité*!' Lizzie repeated.

Lizzie surveyed the Market Square. Dozens of people were already assembled, more adding to the crowd every minute. The last time she had seen so many people in one place was at the Goose Fair last autumn. But today, everyone was there for a different reason. A flock of pigeons circled overhead and the clouds began to separate allowing pale sunshine to illuminate the gaunt faces. Robert greeted his fellow workers. Sam and Joan Elliott had brought all their children, even the youngest son Michael, who was jumping up and down with excitement. Joan took his hand and told him to stand still. One of his older sisters took his other hand, and he swung between the two of them instead.

'Humpty Dumpty sat on a wall, Humpty Dumpty had a great fall,' he sang.

'Is Ben not here?' asked Robert.

Sam Elliott shook his head. 'He had to stay at home with his mother.'

Robert looked bemused. 'With his mother?'

'Between you and me, his uncle doesn't approve of this sort of lark.'

'It didn't stop Ben frame breaking,' Robert whispered.

Sam grunted, 'Well, that's at night, isn't it? This is broad daylight, where everyone can see you. It's nailing your colours to the mast, as they say.'

'Georgie Porgy pudding and pie, kissed the girls and made them cry!' Michael sang.

Robert laughed. He exchanged a look with Sam, 'Right little rebel that one, isn't he?' Robert grinned at Michael, he crouched down and wiggled his fingers at him. Michael giggled and waved back.

'Where he gets it from, I don't know,' Joan said, nudging her husband.

'Runs in the family,' Sam said. He nodded to the roll of

fabric Robert was holding, 'What's that?'

'It's a flag. Lets open it; then we can carry it.' Lizzie and Robert unrolled it.

'Look at that!' Sam was impressed. 'Says it all, don't it?' Robert looked around. The crowd was enormous. 'What do we do now?' Sam asked.

'Blowed if I know.' Robert turned to Lizzie: 'What do you reckon?'

She stood on tiptoe. 'There are other people with signs,' she said. 'There's a man holding a board that says *Pity our children*.'

'Amen to that,' Joan murmured.

'We must have someone to get us all to move as one. We could march up the square,' Lizzie suggested, 'then everyone who's not a stockinger will see what we're up to.'

Robert let go of the sheet. 'You hang on to this and I'll see if I can get everyone's attention.'

'Good luck,' Sam said.

Robert pushed his way out of the throng. He beckoned to Lizzie, Sam and Joan to bring the banner forward. They spread it out across the front of the crowd. When other people saw what it said, they smiled in agreement. One rather tall woman pushed to the front to help carry it.

'That's bloody marvellous!' she exclaimed.

Robert waved his hands and gradually the crowd quieted. He cupped his hands round his mouth and shouted, 'Can every body hear me?'

'No!' one man shouted, and a few people laughed.

Robert yelled, 'WE ALL KNOW WHY WE ARE HERE. IF WE MARCH UP THE SQUARE AND BACK, WE CAN SHOW THE GOOD PEOPLE OF NOTTINGHAM OUR PLIGHT. WE ARE ALL SUFFERING. WE ARE ALL STARVING!' He paused for a moment then began the chant, 'GIVE - US - BREAD!' 'GIVE - US - BREAD!' The crowd took up the cry. They began to walk towards the Castle end of the square. Robert rejoined his sister and resumed chanting as the entire crowd moved as one, Joan and Sam, with their children at one end of the banner, Lizzie and Robert in the middle, and the tall woman at the other.

The Elliott children started singing, 'Pity the children, pity the children, we - have nowt - to eat! Pity the children, pity the children, we - have nowt - to eat!' soon accompanied by Michael singing 'Georgie Porgy' over and over again.

Lizzie could feel a sense of urgency welling within her, as over a thousand people all chanted and moved in one direction. She turned to Robert: 'If we were in London,' she said, 'we could march on the palace. There are so many of us.'

Robert grinned. 'I know; we could take over the country.'

Lizzie's eyes widened. 'This is what happened in France, isn't it?'

Before Robert could answer, someone shouted, 'The army's here!'

Panic rippled through the crowd. 'Don't run!' she shouted. 'They can't do anything to us; there are women and children here.'

Robert looked unconvinced. 'I don't think they care. All they'll see is a mob.'

Sam and Joan gathered their children together. Michael stopped singing for a moment, sensing something was wrong.

An officer on horseback cantered around the outside of the crowd, herding them like sheep. The tall woman that had been carrying the banner made gestures at him.

'Find some soldiers to fight, you coward!' she screamed.

He reared his horse and people flinched. He waved his arm, beckoning, and a flank of soldiers jogged forward, their rifles cocked, bayonets glinting.

'Jesus!' Robert exclaimed, 'They're never going to charge us?'

Some in the crowd scattered and a group of soldiers chased them. Another wave of militia followed, and this time the entire group was surrounded. Infantry three men deep hemmed them in.

'We're trapped!' Lizzie cried.

'HOLD YOUR GROUND!' Robert shouted, 'EVERYONE, STAY STILL!'

Joan's eldest daughter Caroline took Lizzie's arm. 'Do they mean to kill us?' she gasped.

Lizzie shook her head. 'No, no we'll be safe.' But her voice trembled; she was terrified. She put her arm around the young girl's shoulders.

'I'm frightened,' Caroline whispered.

'So am I,' admitted Robert.

The crowd lurched from side to side as the militia penned them, crushing them together.

'I can't breathe,' Sam gasped.

'This is madness!' Robert elbowed his way out to the edge: 'OY!' he shouted, 'You dogs! Threatening your own people! You should be ashamed of yourselves!' He caught the eye of the soldier closest to him and managed to get hold of his rifle. 'You should be on our side; you're only paid a pittance, like us! You're no different!'

'Hands off the weapon, sir, or I'll arrest you,' the soldier growled.

'Let *us* go; we've done nothing wrong!' Robert yelled.

At that moment, the officer rode toward him. He cocked his pistol and aimed it at Robert's head.

'Robert!' Lizzie screeched. She pushed toward him and placed herself between Robert and the gun.

'Stand aside, Madam!' the officer barked.

'I'll not! You'll have to shoot me as well.' She could feel hot tears in her eyes. Robert's chest heaved behind her. A moment of silence seemed to last an age. Lizzie shut her eyes, waiting for the shot. The officer raised his pistol in the air and fired. He bellowed at the crowd: 'DISPERSE IMMEDIATELY! YOU HAVE BEEN WARNED. IF

YOU DO NOT DISPERSE, WE SHALL USE ALL THE FORCE OF HIS MAJESTY'S MILITIA: YOU HAVE BEEN WARNED!'

The soldiers stepped back one pace and aimed their rifles. The people ran, dropping placards and fleeing from the square in terror. Joan and Sam took their children's hands and fled, the children in tears, all except Michael who was defiantly singing 'Georgie Porgy' again.

Lizzie opened her eyes; she swallowed hard. She and Robert looked on, as the soldiers who were still facing the square, with fixed bayonets, waited to charge anyone insubordinate. Once the crowd had broken up, the soldiers formed ranks and marched up and down the square. People wearing their best clothes, out for a Sunday stroll, had witnessed the entire spectacle; a bizarre scene for the Sabbath in Nottingham's Market Square. The soldiers then marched back up the Derby Road, towards the barracks.

Robert caught his breath. His foot touched something on the ground. It was the cloth banner. Lizzie picked it up. She folded it into a square and held it to her breast. She reached out to Robert and hugged him. He sobbed, 'That's why there will never be a revolution in this country; it's *cassé*, divided. There is no Bonaparte here.'

JULY 1811

The young man sighed as his carriage drew to a halt in the courtyard. Catching sight of his reflection in the coach window, he saw how his cheeks had already lost their suntanned glow. His dark hair now felt too long. He stepped down and gazed around him. The lake was the same leaden grey, and the gaping arch of the empty abbey window yawned a greeting to him. Two years. Two years since he had been home. How much was the same, but how much had changed. He shivered. The English summer weather would be winter in the countries from which he had just returned; the places he had described in his poetry. His thoughts ran to what John Murray had said in London: 'You have found your own voice.' His musings on his travels were appreciated, his writing was approved, ready for publication, ready for an audience.

A loud clatter broke his reverie as his stout servant heaved luggage from the coach.

'Careful, Fletcher, there are fragile jars in there.'

'Sorry, m'lord.' Fletcher slowly dragged the case towards the abbey steps.

'Let me see.' The young man indicated for him to open the box. Fletcher unfastened the lid.

'No harm done, fortunately.' Nestling amongst straw, the jars of Greek olives and Turkish rose oil were intact. The perfume had been intended as a gift for his mother. He swallowed; she would not need it now. He blinked away his tears and drew a deep breath.

'Take it inside,' he ordered.

'Yes, m'lord.' Fletcher did not need him to explain. Over the last two years he had come to know his employer's moods. The valet knew when to speak and when to remain silent.

Fletcher watched as his master glided with ease through the glass-green water of the lake. He had reached the far bank, sunshine gilding the waves in his wake. The servant squinted in the bright light. It was the warmest day they'd had since coming home. He shielded his eyes with his hand. The young man had clambered out of the water on the far side of the lake. Fletcher observed his master climb onto the turret on the furthest shore; he stretched and then dived back into the cool waves.

'He's like a fish,' Fletcher said to himself, smiling. 'His lordship swims and drinks like a fish.'

Suddenly he was aware of a sound, a dog barking. He turned and saw a scruffy, red-haired hound limping out of the woods. 'Who are you?' he asked. He placed the clothes and towels he was holding on the ground and walked over to the dog. As he came closer, it seemed more like a wolf. He stepped forward cautiously. 'Don't worry, lad, I'll not hurt you.' The dog looked dejected. Its paw was raised in pain. 'You've most likely got a splinter.' The animal gave a mournful whine. Fletcher noticed it had no collar, and its coat was rough and unkempt. He knelt down and examined the dog's paw. There was a thorn stuck between the pads. 'Hold steady, I'll help you.' He gripped the thorn with his fingers and tugged it out. The dog yelped. The servant patted him. 'That's better, in't it?' The dog gingerly placed its paw on the ground.

'Have you abandoned me for a crippled beast?'

Fletcher turned to see his master, still dripping wet from his swim, a towel wrapped round his waist.

'I'm sorry, m'lord,' he explained, 'he had a thorn in his paw.'

The young man smiled. 'His need was greater than mine.' He crouched down to the dog and stroked it. 'No collar. You belong to no one. You are a limping wanderer, as I am.'

In the heat, the dog was panting, eyes fixed on his new master.

'I can dress myself, Fletcher. Take this wounded wolf inside. Give him plenty of water, and whatever there is to feed him, let him have it.'

'Very good, m'lord.' Fletcher walked to the courtyard, and turning to the animal, he said, 'Come on then, lad.' He patted his thigh and the dog followed him toward the kitchen. The young lord watched as they disappeared into the abbey. He returned to the lakeside and retrieved his clothes, pausing for a while to enjoy the sunshine. His silver-blue eyes watched swifts swiping their supper as they swooped overhead. He removed his towel and arranged it on the ground. He sat down and addressed the lake: 'You are not the Hellespont, but I have missed you,' he sighed, 'I love and hate this country in equal measure.'

Peter Connor drew the brush over the horse's back, its bristles forming neat rows. The stallion shivered a little and swung its tail. Connor patted its neck.

'There, boy; nearly finished.' He took a comb and separated the chestnut fronds of its mane. Engrossed in his task, he did not hear his employer enter the stable.

'I must say, Mr Connor, my horses are looking fine. You care for them expertly.'

Connor bowed. 'Glad to do so, m'lord.'

The young man patted the horse's neck. 'I mean to ride to Hucknall tomorrow, to collect the rent from the estate. Will you see that my Bucephalus is prepared for the morning?'

Connor nodded. 'What time would your lordship want to leave?'

'You know I am not an early riser,' the young man said, smiling. 'Ten-thirty should be adequate.'

Connor combed the horse's tail. 'Begging your lordship's pardon, but what name did you call him?'

'Bucephalus.'

'I thought so,' Connor said. 'Wasn't that the name of Alexander The Great's horse?'

'Indeed it was! The finest leader the Greeks ever had.' His eyes shone. 'How have you encountered the great hero?'

'I was in the army, m'lord. All soldiers have heard of Alexander. He led from the front, not sitting on a hill half a mile away.' He gave a rueful laugh. The young lord smiled.

'Indeed. Modern warfare appears to be a contest as to which side has the most cannon-fodder.' He paused. 'Why did you leave the army?' he finally asked.

'Got shot in the foot. Well, a shard of metal went through my foot, I should say. Couldn't march any more. Added to that, I wanted to be at home with my family. Didn't like the idea of Jack growing up without a father.'

'How old is he?'

'Seventeen now; and I'd shoot him in the foot rather than see him go for a soldier. Not much chance of that though,' Connor chuckled. 'He's too busy chasing girls.'

The young man laughed. At that moment, a youth appeared at the stable door, with a pretty girl on his arm.

'I was just talking about you,' Connor said. The lad noticed his father's employer and bowed. 'Afternoon, m'lord.'

'Good afternoon. Your father was informing me of

your romantic exploits.' He eyed the girl.

'This is Susan, your lordship.' The girl stepped from his side and curtseyed. A knowing smile appeared on the nobleman's lips.

'I am presently seeking maidservants for the Abbey. Do you think you would accept an offer of employment?'

Susan exchanged a look with Jack. She was a few years older than her lover, and her olive-coloured eyes expressed her more advanced experience.

'It would be an honour, my lord.' Her accent had an unexpected Welsh lilt.

'What a charming voice you have!' He took her hand and kissed it. Jack looked uncomfortable, but said nothing.

'That's settled then. You may begin this afternoon, if you wish. Mr Fletcher will explain your duties; he's my valet. I only have two commandments: first, you shall not wake me before ten o'clock in the morning unless I have expressly requested it, or there is some emergency of Biblical proportions, like a fire or a flood. I do keep unusual hours, as no doubt Mr Fletcher will also inform you. And secondly, you must be available at all times, is that clear?' His eyes met hers, unblinking. Susan nodded.

'I understand m'lord.'

'Good,' he said. 'And one thing further: I will have no caps or topknots, so leave your hair unbound—as it is now.'

He turned to Connor: 'Tomorrow, ten-thirty.'

'The horse will be ready m'lord.'

'I will see you later, Susan.' With that he left the stable.

Jack met Susan's gaze. 'What?' she asked.

'What did he mean about being available...at all times?'

Susan stroked her fingers through Jack's light brown hair. 'You heard him; he keeps odd hours is all.' She kissed him.

Connor resumed grooming the horse. Susan stroked Jack's cheek. 'I'm sure I'll have some time off, so I can still serve *you*.' The young lad blushed. 'Come on,' Susan said between kisses, 'let's fetch my things.'

Connor watched them leave. He gave a rueful smile. *Droit de seigneur*,' he murmured to the horse, 'that's what his lordship meant.'

AUGUST 1811

*J*oan Elliott showed Lizzie into the bedroom. Lizzie removed her shawl and sat next to the bed.

'How long has he been like this?'

'Since yesterday evening. He said he felt sick. Wouldn't touch his supper.'

Lizzie stroked the little boy's forehead. 'He's hot. He has a fever.' She leaned close to him. She could hear his rapid breath. She prayed it was not too late. 'What has he had to eat?'

'Porridge yesterday morning, that's all.'

'Are you sure? Did he go out of the house?'

Joan looked worried. 'The older ones went berrying. He went with them, but he came back not long after.'

'Why was that?'

'He said it was too hot. He's never liked the sun. What can we do, Lizzie?'

Lizzie placed her fingers gently against Michael's neck. She could feel his pulse. It was fast, but strong. She carefully opened his mouth a little so that she could see his tongue. It was swollen. 'I think he might have eaten a poisonous berry. And he has sunstroke.'

Joan sank onto a chair. 'Poisoned?'

'Get a small towel, boil it and bring it to me. If he's hot, we must cool him; if he's cold, we need to warm him.' Lizzie took Joan's hand. 'Don't be afraid. He's strong, he's fighting it.'

They returned to the kitchen. Lizzie opened her bag on the table and took out little jars containing dried leaves and herbs. 'Boil some water and I'll make him some tea.'

Joan looked at the herbs. 'What sort of tea is that?'

'They're herbs that heal,' Lizzie reassured her. 'Fennel; will cool him, and Valerian will help him sleep.'

Joan put a kettle on to boil. Then she placed a tea towel in a copper saucepan filled with water and heated it over the fire. When it was hot, she removed the towel with a wooden laundry pincer and hung it near the mantle. Lizzie warmed the teapot with a little hot water, then added the herbs and filled it.

'While that's mashing, I'll wash his hands and face.' She took the towel to the bedroom. Lizzie sat next to the bed once more. She gently wiped Michael's face, washing away the sweat on his brow. She cleaned both his hands, hoping that any traces of poison were gone. She gently bolstered him upright with another pillow. Lizzie returned to the kitchen and brought the tea to him in a small jug. She lifted it to his lips.

'Michael, try to drink this for me. It will taste bitter, but it will help you. Will you try?' He did not respond. Lizzie turned to Joan. 'He's faint.'

Joan wrung her hands. 'I'll do anything to help him.'

'Michael!' Lizzie said his name more loudly. His eyes flickered open. He frowned. 'It's Lizzie. Will you drink this? It'll make you better.'

'Lizzie?' He whispered.

'Yes, your mother is here as well. Will you try?'

Michael nodded slowly. Lizzie brought the jug to his lips. She helped him sip the bitter tea. After he had drunk about half of it, Lizzie let him lie back once more. 'Well done,' she said.

'It's horrible,' Michael whispered.

'I know. You'll feel better later, though, I promise.'

Joan sat next to the bed. She stroked his forehead. She turned to Lizzie and wiped tears away with her apron. 'Will he live?' she whispered.

Lizzie turned to her. 'He's strong. How old is he?'

Joan shivered. 'Six. I've lost all three babies younger than him.'

Lizzie crossed herself.

'The others are all older. Sam's taken them to church, to pray for him.' Joan sobbed. 'Lizzie, I can't lose him, my little angel Michael.'

Lizzie stood and put her arms around Joan. She felt as though she were her mother. 'You and Samuel are good parents.' She stroked her hair. 'You're exhausted. Did you sleep last night?' Joan shook her head. 'Please, go and lie down, get some sleep. I'll wake you if he gets worse, I promise.'

Joan wiped her eyes and settled herself on her bed. Lizzie lifted the blanket over her and returned to Michael's bedside. She drew out her rosary and began to pray.

The candle had burned half its height when Lizzie realised that she too had begun to doze, her rosary in her lap. She had been dreaming. She was by a huge river. Had she been gathering herbs? Next to the river was an enormous, sandstone coloured building, much bigger than St Mary's church. She yawned. Michael now reminded her of Robert: many years ago he'd had a fever, and on her father's instruction she had fetched the herbs from the dresser. She had watched as Papa brewed them into tea and made Robert drink. Despite his illness, Robert had been powerfully reluctant. Papa said that *Maman* had known how to use herbs properly, but he could only remember a few medicines, and that Lizzie was not to tell anyone, especially the priest, because he would not understand. The remedy had worked and Robert was soon been back on his feet and getting into mischief. Lizzie replaced the rosary round her neck and looked over at Joan, who was fast asleep. Michael was now blinking, looking around.

'Lizzie?' His voice was quiet and hoarse. 'Where's everyone gone? Where's Mama?'

'She's asleep,' Lizzie whispered.

'Oh. Where's Papa? Where are the others?'

'They've gone to church.'

'Why aren't I there?'

'You're not very well. You've had to stay here.'

'It was too hot. The sun was too bright.' Michael frowned.

'Yesterday?'

'Yes. We found some blackberries though. I found some secret berries. I'll tell you where they are.'

'Those berries, did you eat them?'

Michael nodded. 'Was that wrong?'

'They made you very ill.' Lizzie squeezed his hand. 'Don't ever eat them again, will you?'

'No. They were horrible. I'm thirsty now though, and hungry.'

Lizzie gave him some more of the tea.

'Can I have something to eat?'

Lizzie smiled. 'What would you like?'

'Roast potatoes. Will you ask Mama?' He looked over at his mother. 'Don't wake her yet. It's nice, just us here, being quiet. A lot of the time it's too noisy and there're too many people.'

Lizzie stroked his forehead.

'Do you know any songs?' he asked. Lizzie nodded. 'Will you sing me a song?'

'Would you like me to sing a song in French for you?'

'Yes, please.' Michael smiled.

Softly Lizzie sang:

'*Une petite souris verte, qui couris sous l'herbe, je l'attrape par la queue, je la montre à ces monsieurs, ces monsieurs me disent, tombez-elle dans l'huile, et elle fait un escargot, tout chaud.'*

'What does it mean?'

Lizzie translated. Michael laughed quietly. 'I've never seen a green mouse, have you?'

Lizzie smiled. 'No, I haven't.'

'Why would you want to make it into a snail?'

'To eat it.'

'Do they eat snails in France?'

'Sometimes.'

Michael wrinkled his nose. 'I don't think I should like that. Would you?'

'I don't know; I've never eaten one.'

'I'd rather have roast potatoes,' Michael said with some certainty.

As Lizzie looked round, Joan was standing at the end of the bed. She sat next to Michael and kissed him. 'You can have as many roast potatoes as you like.' She looked at Lizzie. 'Thank you,' she said.

'Lizzie sang a song to me in French,' Michael said.

'What?' Joan looked confused.

'It was, wasn't it?' He looked at Lizzie. She nodded.

Joan patted Michael's hand. 'You go back to sleep now. You'll feel better in the morning. Say good-bye to Lizzie.'

Lizzie stood up and Joan ushered her to the kitchen. She closed the door to the bedroom. Lizzie was shocked by the hostility in Joan's eyes.

'I'm sorry, he asked me to sing a song to him,' she began.

'I don't want you teaching my children French songs, or anything else French. He's just a little boy; he doesn't understand. I don't know what you might be telling him.'

'It was just a nursery rhyme.' Lizzie met Joan's eyes: 'It's nothing terrible. You trust me, don't you?'

Joan looked unsure.

'You trusted me with the herbs. You know I can help you. I'd never do anything to hurt you or your children.'

Lizzie gathered her things. 'I've lived in Nottingham since I was five years old. My father brought us here because all he wanted was for his children to be safe. That's all any parent wants, isn't it?'

Joan nodded. 'Of course...'

Lizzie took Joan's hand. 'I would never do you any harm. I promise.' Lizzie picked up her shawl and wrapped it round her shoulders. 'Will Sam and the girls be home soon?'

Joan nodded. 'I'd better go. Robert will be wanting his supper.'

Joan opened the door to let Lizzie out. She paused for a moment then said, 'Thank you, Lizzie.'

Lizzie stopped herself from saying '*De rien.*' Instead she said, 'You're welcome.'

SEPTEMBER 1811

Right pedal, the thread rattled its way across the frame. Left pedal; lock up the jacks. Robert could do it in his sleep. Half the time he thought he was asleep. His mind wandered back to the summer: the protest in the square, the officer pointing the pistol at him. Robert tried to think of something more pleasant; the azure sky, the warm sun on his face at the fair. Lizzie trying to stop him from gambling. Ben taking all the winnings. Sarah... Sarah... The mechanism seemed to mutter her name with every movement.

'Damn it!' he hissed. Had he dropped a stitch? He wasn't concentrating. Robert stopped to check the threading. He straightened the loops back into position. No harm done. He was well ahead.

'Something the matter, Bob?' Mr Betts wandered over to him.

'No, sir. Thought I'd dropped a stitch.'

'Not like you. Not like you at all.' Betts lifted up a pair of stockings from the pile next to Robert's frame. 'Perfect, every one. You crack on like this, lad, and we'll have the

47

order finished in no time.' He sauntered over to Ben. 'You could learn from him, you know. Twice as much he's done.'

Ben kept silent, gritting his teeth.

'You're almost as bad as Mr Elliott,' Betts teased, 'isn't he, Sam?'

Samuel Elliott didn't answer; engrossed in his work he knew better than to listen to conversation that might put him off.

'He's concentrating. You could learn from him, Ben. Sam might be slow, but he's steady.'

Robert glanced over at Ben who by this time was seething.

'If you put as much energy into your work as you do into gambling and drinking, then you'd be as much a machine as Molyneux, here.'

Robert looked down at his work. The less said about drinking and gambling the better, he thought.

Dusk was already gathering when the men filed out of the workshop. Leaves danced in the chilly air. The paving stones were greasy with leaf mulch. Robert shuddered: the fading light and dying plants gave him a feeling of melancholy as the last ray of the sun was obscured by a leaden cloud.

'I'm sick of him going on like that.' Ben kicked a stone. Robert had to double his pace to keep up with Ben's long strides.

'I know; it's my fault. If I hadn't said anything when I thought I'd dropped a stitch—'

'It's not you. Anything sets him off.' Ben gave Robert a sideways glance. 'Bloody annoying that you're so fast, though. I'll never be good enough for my frigging uncle.'

They turned up Stoney Street. 'I could murder him,' Ben spat. 'Ever since my father died, he's taken over completely. He was never going to let me be the next Harwood in the Betts and Harwood business, was he? I shouldn't even be working. He could afford to give me an allowance; I should be a gentleman.' They reached the Angel tavern. Robert stopped in front of the mullioned windows and counted his wages.

'Ay up Bob!' Thomas Jackson appeared, puffing his portly body up Barker Gate. 'You've saved me a walk. I can give you Lizzie's wages while I'm here. That alright?'

Robert nodded. Jackson counted out the wages. His sausage-like fingers slowly placed the coins in Robert's palm, meticulously transferring them one at a time, as though he was bestowing a great gift. 'That's only two shillings' worth each,' Robert said. 'Oh, sorry,' said the pay master, 'I must have a couple of sixpences in the other pocket.' He retrieved the little silver coins and passed them to Robert. 'There you are. I'll collect the rest of her work next week. Struggling to shift them at the moment, you know. There's not the demand for silk stockings now.' He caught his breath. 'Trade'll pick up in the winter, mark you. There's wealthy folks want proper soft stockings to keep their feet warm.' He caught sight of Ben's surly expression. 'What's up with Master Harwood? Cheer up, lad; it might never happen.' Jackson grinned and slapped Ben on the back.

'That's what I'm afraid of,' Ben snarled.

'Eh, well, ne'er mind, duck—soon be Christmas!' With that he bustled off towards Goose Gate, whistling a merry version of 'The First Noel'.

Robert chuckled. 'It's only September.'

Ben caught his eye and laughed: 'Dozy sod!'

Robert pushed open the solid door and a wave of warm air welcomed him. 'Come on, you'll feel better after a few pints.'

'I'll feel better if I spend my wages with Sarah,' Ben smirked.

Robert felt the blood drain from his face. He ran his hands through his hair. The last thing he wanted to think about was Ben having his way with Sarah. Ben yawned.

'Mind you, I'm that flaming tired,' he sniggered, 'I'll probably fall asleep on her.'

Robert's forced laughter sounded hollow.

When Ben and Robert entered The Angel, Emma was pinning up a notice next to the bar. Smoke from the men's long clay pipes swirled across the room, the walls ingrained with stains and fumes. Wooden tables scored with scratches from knives lined the walls; rough boards for draughts or card games carved into the surfaces. The clay pint pots were lined up along the bar, ready for the early customers. Despite the inviting scent of beer and the coal fire, Emma was not her usual convivial self.

'What's this?' Ben leaned closer to read the poster.

'A curfew...' Emma turned to him, 'You've all got to be gone, and I've got to close up, before ten o'clock.'

'Bloody hell!' said Ben.

'I'll not have cursing, if you don't mind.'

'That's rich coming from you,' Ben smirked. 'What happens if we don't go home before then?'

Emma sucked her teeth. 'You get arrested.'

Robert snorted. 'That's ridiculous!'

'Ridiculous it may be, but it's the law, and I'm not going to have my licence taken away.'

Emma's expression was that of a schoolteacher reprimanding small boys. 'I'm old enough to be your mother, Robert Molyneux, and I'll not have you getting yourself into trouble.'

'We best start drinking then,' said Ben 'if we've only got a couple of hours.' He drew out a few coins and placed them on the bar. 'Where's my angel tonight?' he grinned.

'She'll be down in a minute.' Emma filled two tankards with dark foaming ale then resumed cleaning glasses.

Ben and Robert sat at one of the tables. 'If I play my cards well, then I'll not need to worry about curfews.' Ben winked. Robert almost spat out his beer.

'You mean to stay with her?'

'Only for tonight.' He leaned close to Robert and lowered his conspiratorial voice. 'Sarah may look like an angel, but she's a devil in the bedroom. She doesn't charge too much either. You should try her sometime.'

Robert gulped his ale. 'I don't think so,' he said finally.

Ben shook his head. 'You're missing out. She'll do anything. Anything you want.'

Robert looked up and saw Sarah enter the bar. She was more desirable than ever, her hazel eyes bright darts that pierced his heart. Her soft breast, displayed enticingly, rose and fell with each breath.

Ben turned round. 'Here she is; my angel of Hockley!'

'Evening Ben, Robert,' said Sarah, smiling. She settled herself on the bench next to Ben. He coiled his arm around her shoulders then slid his hand down to the steep curve of her waist. Her body reminded Robert of ripe fruit ready to tumble out of her dress at any moment.

'Are you not playing dice or cards tonight?' she asked.

'We've not got long.' Robert nodded at the notice. Sarah raised her eyes. 'I know; it's going to be bad for business, isn't it?'

Ben slipped a coin into her hand. 'A shilling says you won't miss out tonight,' he whispered in her ear. 'And there'll be more than that if I'm lucky.' He took his pack of playing cards from his pocket. 'Why don't we have a quick game of Twenty-One?'

Robert thought of Lizzie. If he could win even one game, then he'd take home double what he'd been paid. He grinned. '*Allons-y!*'

Sarah clapped her hands. 'I love it when you speak French! It makes you seem even more dark and mysterious.' She winked at him.

'*Vous êtes très belle,*' he said with a gallant nod of his head. Sarah giggled. Ben dealt the cards. He stretched his long legs forward.

'That's enough of that foreign talk,' he half smirked at

Robert. 'Don't forget we're at war with your lot.'

Sarah upbraided him. 'Ben! *I'm* not at war with anyone. Anyway, Robert's lived here all his life. He's as much from Notts as you or me.'

Robert blushed as he took up his cards: 'Twist,' he said. He placed a coin on the table. Sarah took a card from the pack and passed it to him. 'Twist.' Another coin. She dealt him his second card. He paused.

'Stick.' Any higher than a two and he'd be bust.

Ben took a card. He smiled. 'Twist,' he said, putting down three coins. Sarah dealt him a card.

'Stick.' He showed no emotion this time, but he needed Robert to lose, or an Ace to reach Twenty-One. Sarah gave another card to Robert.

'Bust,' he sighed.

Ben scooped all the coins off the table. 'Ah, bad luck. I'll buy you another drink as compensation.' He strode over to the bar. Sarah shook her head. 'You're so unlucky, Robert.'

'I don't know what I'm going to do,' he said. 'Lizzie's going to kill me. I promised her I wouldn't gamble any more.'

Sarah could see how upset he was. She leaned closer to him. 'Don't worry, I've got a plan. I'll get your money back for you.' She glanced at Ben over her shoulder. She was sure he couldn't hear her. 'Leave it to me.'

Robert looked at her, curious. Why would she want to help him? Perhaps she cared less for Ben than it appeared. How easily her angelic face hid her scheming nature.

Ben brought three more tankards to the table and set them down. 'Thank you,' said Sarah. She kissed him. Ben drew Sarah's face to his and kissed her again, closing his eyes. Sarah's gaze, however, met Robert's, and she gave him a licentious look.

Robert gulped the last of his ale. 'I'd better be off,' he said.

'So soon?' said Ben. 'Then give Lizzie my best, won't

you?' He smiled and returned to kissing Sarah. Robert left them to it. As he made his way along the dark streets, he decided he would not tell Lizzie about his misfortune, but rather wait until Sarah had followed her stratagem.

Emma cleared away the last of the pewter tankards and wiped down the bar. Only Sarah and Ben remained. Sarah stood up and tiptoed over to her.

'Emma,' she wheedled, 'if I give you an extra sixpence for my lodging, can you look the other way tonight?' She glanced over at Ben, who was counting his coins. Emma sighed, but took the sixpence. 'You be careful, girl. As long as he's gone before I open up tomorrow lunchtime, I don't care what you get up to.'

'Thanks Emma,' said Sarah. 'There's not many landladies would be so understanding.'

Emma watched as Sarah led Ben up the stairs, then she snuffed out the lamps in the bar and made her way to her own rooms at the back of the pub.

As soon as they were in Sarah's room, Ben pulled off his coat and flung it over a chair. Then he caught Sarah around the waist and pressed her mouth with a hasty kiss.

'Are your winnings burning a hole in your pocket?' she asked.

'That's not the only thing,' he said between his rough kisses.

'Do you want to spend it?' she asked, unbuttoning his breeches.

'Oh, I want to spend alright.' He pushed her onto the bed. 'What will you do for two shillings?' he asked, tossing all his coins on her table.

'Whatever you want,' she said, lying back on the pillows.

Ben unbuttoned his shirt and turned away briefly as he threw it on the floor. Sarah noticed that the familiar scars on his back were mottled with fresh bruises. He sat on the bed. 'Hit me!' he said. She slapped him on the cheek.

'Harder!' She did it again. 'More!' he ordered. She did so even more firmly. Ben grinned. He unwound the cotton scarf from his throat and threaded it through the top bedpost. Then he pushed Sarah's arms up over her head and tied both her wrists to the post. He lifted her skirts to reveal her solid legs.

'Tell me to stop,' he said.

'Stop,' Sarah giggled.

'I don't believe you want me to,' he said. 'Say it again.'

'Stop!' she cried.

'That's better.' He climbed on top of her, kissing her roughly, pushing her legs apart with his own. She cried out again. 'That's good,' he said, sliding her knees up. He tore at her dress and gripped her breasts.

Downstairs Emma could hear Sarah's bed creaking with increasing rhythm. Suddenly it stopped. Ben withdrew. He loosened the scarf from Sarah's wrists. She was relieved, as it was starting to hurt a little.

'What do you want to do now?' she gasped.

'Tie me up,' he said. 'Then fuck me.'

She tied his right hand to one bed post and used one of her own stockings to secure the other. She straddled him.

'Scratch me!' he ordered. She dragged her nails down his chest. 'Harder!' he said. She could feel him grow more aroused with every scratch. She became more excited herself. Soon his cries matched hers and they shuddered to a loud climax. 'You may look like an angel, Sarah, but you fuck like a demon,' he growled.

Sarah laughed. 'You're no saint, neither, Ben.' She climbed off him and began to pick up the coins. In the dark she could feel there was far more than three shillings. She silently slid them off the table and into her little leather purse. She looked out the window at the lopsided moon, clouds rushing across its bony face. She thought about Robert and how he'd lost the card game. Then she realised: Ben hadn't shuffled the cards. He'd cheated.

'Untie me now,' Ben demanded.

'I will,' she said, 'as long as you add another shilling to what you've paid me.'

Ben's face grew sullen. 'Just do it,' he snapped.

'You've torn my dress as well. It'll cost me to mend it.'

Ben tugged at his bonds but knew she would have to release him.

'Go on then, take it!'

Sarah smiled. 'Thank you.' She untied one of Ben's hands as he caught hold of her wrist. 'Don't meddle with me like this again.' His voice was harsh.

'You asked me to tie you up.'

'You know what I mean,' he said. He untied his other hand himself. Then he grabbed her.

'What are you doing?' she asked.

He pushed her back down on to the bed. She tried to fight him off, but he was strong. His long legs parted hers. He held her hands firmly. A cruel smile appeared on his lips.

'Tell me to stop,' he said.

'No!' she cried.

'Say it!'

Sarah tried to turn her face away. He kissed her. His mouth was hard, his kisses like bites.

'Now I'm going to get what I've paid for,' he whispered.

OCTOBER 1811

'I've got to make reductions. The expenditure is greater than the income. That's not business, it's madness.' Mr Betts leaned forward over his desk. Robert and Sam stood before him. Sunshine crept over the office floorboards, glinting on the brass inkwells. Robert noticed a tiny spider teetering along the edge of the table. 'I'm sorry, lads, but I've made as many cuts as I can.' His hands ran over the ledger. 'I don't like this cheap work any more than you do, but it's the way things are heading,' Betts shuffled the papers on his desk. 'We need to be profitable. The main market's abroad now.' He looked from one to the other: 'There's no other way of putting this; one of you has got to go.'

Sam Elliott gave an audible gasp. Robert met his employer's gaze.

'I'll go, sir. I've got no family to support. My sister can earn enough for both of us. We'll manage.'

Betts clicked his tongue. 'You think so? I doubt it. I'm not going to lose one of my most productive workers. No, I'm sorry, but Mr Elliott, it has to be you.'

Sam was dumbstruck. He squeezed his cap in his hands with white knuckles. Robert spoke again: 'Sir, have pity; he's got seven children to feed.'

Mr Betts looked down. 'That's unfortunate. But I'm afraid it's not up to me to be charitable. I'm a businessman.'

Robert could see that Sam was shaking; his narrow face deathly pale. Robert rubbed his chin. 'Couldn't you keep us both on with less wages? Or, I'll work three days and he'll work the other three?'

Betts shook his head. 'No, that won't do, won't do at all. If trade doesn't pick up, you'll only be working three days anyway, and you'll all be on half wages.'

Robert paused for a moment as he digested the threat. He could feel a knot of anger in his chest. 'And what if we refuse to do that? What if we all just stopped working until you relent?'

Betts stood and fixed Robert's stare. 'Have a care, Master Molyneux. You're a good worker, but you're not indispensable. Going 'on strike', a mutiny as the sailors call it, is against the law.'

'Then the law's wrong,' Robert hissed.

Betts took out his pocket watch, 'Four o'clock. I suggest you both finish for today and think about what I've said.' He drew out a small key and opened a tin box. He removed a handful of coins. 'Here you are, Mr Elliott, a week's wages. That should tide you over until you find other employment.'

Sam slowly placed the coins in his pocket. His voice was a timid whisper: 'Thank you, sir.'

Robert shook his head. He took Sam's arm for fear he might collapse and silently led him out of the workshop.

Glints of sunlight sparkled through the trees; shadows fluttered over the gravestones. Sam and Robert sat on the churchyard wall.

'He can't do it,' Robert asserted. 'It's wrong!'

Sam's eyebrows knitted together. 'What am I going to tell Joan?'

'Don't tell her, not yet.' Robert watched a carrion crow pecking at a dead mouse.

'I can't lie to her,' Sam said.

'It's not lying; I'll talk to Betts again tomorrow, try to reason with him. Maybe I could get Ben to speak with him. We must be able to do something.'

'No, Bob. Betts won't change his mind, and I've got to be honest with my wife.'

St Mary's chimed half past four.

'Emma will be opening soon.' Robert checked the change in his pocket. 'I can buy us some drinks. Help you to forget about it.'

Sam said to Robert, 'Getting drunk isn't going to solve anything. Joan knows I don't drink. How do you think she'd like that? Sacked and soused on the same day.' He gazed ahead. 'I've let her down; I've let my family down.'

Robert shivered. 'You could always have supper with us. Lizzie will make enough for three. If you don't want ale, the least we could do is offer you some tea.'

Sam placed his hand on Robert's shoulder. 'That's kind of you, but I must face up to it,' he sighed. 'You go on. I'm going to sit here for a bit and try to think what to say to Joan.'

Robert stood up. 'It'll be getting dark soon,' he said. 'Don't stay out too late. If you change your mind, you know where we live.'

'Where's Papa?'

'I don't know, Caroline. Maybe he had to stay late at the workshop.'

Joan cleared the children's plates from the table and took them to the scullery. The Elliotts' eldest daughter lifted the kettle from the fire and began to make tea.

Joan called from the kitchen, 'Rose, get Michael ready for bed.'

'Yes, Mama.' Rose sat Michael on her knee and began to brush his hair.

'I'm still hungry,' he said.

'We all are,' Caroline said as she poured tea for them.

'I don't want tea, I want hot milk,' Michael moaned.

'*I want* doesn't get,' Joan said as she wiped her hands on her apron, 'Ellie and Mary, plait each other's hair. Don't do it too tight, Ellie.'

The little girls turned around on the bench so they faced each other and began to twist their hair into thick braids.

'There isn't any milk, is there?'

Caroline turned to her younger sister, 'No, Sophie, we can't afford it.'

'We can't afford anything. We'll be drinking hot water and living on fresh air soon.'

'Hush now.' Caroline sat down and looked up at her mother. Joan's expression was worried.

'Is Papa a frame breaker?'

'No Dora, he isn't.' Joan gulped her tea. All the children looked at Dora. She shrugged her shoulders and said, 'I just thought it might explain where he was.' She rubbed her eyes.

Michael squealed, 'Mama! Rose is pulling my hair.'

'I'm not. Don't be such a baby.' Rose pinched him.

'You're all too tired. You're going to bed, right now!' Joan clapped her hands. All the Elliott children stood up.

'I haven't finished plaiting Mary's hair,' said Ellie.

'That's because you were too slow.' Mary tugged her sister's plaits.

'If I do it fast, you moan it's too tight.'

'Enough!' cried Joan, 'Bed! Now!'

'Yes Mama.' Caroline shepherded the others into the bedroom. 'Make sure you fold your clothes properly,' she said, 'or there'll be a slap for anyone who leaves things in a mess.'

Joan gave a grateful glance to her daughter and sat

down at the table. St Mary's chimed eight o'clock. There was a muffled argument in the bedroom which was quelled by Caroline ordering everyone to kneel down and say their prayers. Joan whispered the words along with her children: 'Now I lay me down to sleep, I pray the Lord my soul to keep. If I should die before I wake, I pray the Lord my soul to take.'

Caroline blew out the candle.

Sam unlocked the door and moved with silent steps into his house. He gazed round the kitchen then sank into a chair in front of the dying embers and watched the glowing remains of the fire. There was no wood in the basket next to the grate.

Sam sighed, 'I'm so useless; I forgot to bring firewood.' He ran his hands through his hair. Reaching into his pocket for his handkerchief, he found the coins that Betts had given him for his last wages. He placed them on the table and turned toward the fireplace. Small flames crackled in the grate. Sam took the poker from the fireside and stirred the last of the coal, and tiny sparks jumped from the greying scraps. His thoughts ran unbidden. What could he do? There was no other work for which he was capable, and at his age he'd be hard pushed to find something that paid him enough to feed his children. Betts was a hard man, unrelenting. Sam wished he could have spoken out—or hit him—but he knew he could never raise his fist against anyone. It was good of Robert to speak up on his behalf; he was impulsive but always a kind, and his heart was in the right place. Sam twisted his wedding ring. What was he going to tell Joan? So many years they'd been together: she'd stuck by him, borne his children, always made sure they were washed and fed. The pretty young girl he'd wed in St Mary's was now tired and careworn. It was his fault: she deserved better. 'Til death us do part,' he murmured. A tear fell from his eye onto his shirt.

Hanging on the hearth were several pairs of stockings, the smaller ones belonging to his children, the longer ones that were Joan's. He took one of these and stretched it between his hands.

'Better off without me, you will be,' he muttered. 'At least you'll get money from the Parish. Your mother will find a better man to be your father.'

Lizzie opened her eyes. It was still dark. Half asleep, she became aware of a sound, a fierce knocking at the door. She pushed back the bedclothes and her feet found her slippers on the cold floor. She tiptoed over to Robert and nudged his shoulder.

'Robert,' she hissed. He snored. 'Robert!' She shook him awake.

'What is it?' he said. 'God, Lizzie, what time is it? Am I late?'

'No, there's someone knocking on the door.'

Robert pulled on his jacket over his nightshirt as they both moved into the kitchen. Robert opened the door. A young girl stood outside.

'Caroline Elliott?'

Wearing a shawl over her nightgown, her boots had been hastily pulled on over her bare feet. The girl was hysterical. 'It's Papa!' she cried.

'Come in, you'll freeze to death,' said Lizzie as she ushered Caroline into the kitchen.

Robert lit a candle. 'What's happened to Sam?' he asked.

As Caroline sobbed, Lizzie placed her arm around the girl's shoulders.

'He's dead. Oh Lord, he's dead!'

'Dead?' Robert was incredulous. 'I spoke to him only this afternoon.'

Caroline's eyes were red from crying. 'He's hanged himself.'

Robert and Lizzie crossed themselves.

'He didn't come home. We all went to bed. When Mama woke up in the night— ' The girl broke off and shook.

Lizzie held her. 'Take your time,' she whispered. She exchanged a look with Robert.

'Why did he do it?' sobbed Caroline.

Robert sat down. 'This is Betts' fault.'

'What do you mean?' Lizzie asked.

'Betts dismissed Sam this afternoon.'

'Dismissed?'

Robert nodded. 'I begged him not to. I was going to speak to him again today, tell him that I'd leave rather than see Sam out of work.'

'You didn't tell me any of this,' Lizzie said as she looked into Robert's eyes. She took a cloth from the fireside and gently wiped Caroline's face, drying her tears. Caroline clung to her.

'Mama told me to fetch the vicar, but I couldn't wake him. I knocked on his door but there was no answer. So I came to you.'

Lizzie nodded. 'You did the right thing.' She guided Caroline to a chair. 'Are you able to wait for Robert and I to dress? We'll come home with you.' The girl nodded. The twins dressed quickly, Lizzie placed the candle in a lantern and they made their way to the Elliotts' house.

All the Elliott children were in the kitchen. Michael was once more sitting on Rose's knee. Dora and Sophie sat, like bookends, on a bench. Ellie and Mary occupied themselves plaiting each other's hair.

Caroline showed Lizzie and Robert inside. Michael jumped off Rose's knee: 'Lizzie!' he cried and hugged her. 'Mama won't let us go into the bedroom. Why?'

Lizzie stroked his head.

'Where's Papa?' he asked.

Caroline took Michael's hand and led him back to the table: 'Sit down,' she said.

The little boy looked confused. 'Why is everyone sad?'

Lizzie tapped on the bedroom door. 'Joan, it's Lizzie and Robert.' She opened the door and they entered. Joan was sitting on the floor next to her husband. He was slumped at the bottom of the bed. His face was an almost unrecognisable grimace. A stocking around his throat, he had threaded the noose through the bedpost.

'Jesus!' Robert whispered. He crossed himself again.

Lizzie crouched next to Joan and took her hand. 'Do you think you can stand? You must go to your children.'

Joan stared at her, eyes unblinking.

'Your children need you.'

Joan nodded in silence. Lizzie helped her to her feet. She wandered through and Caroline closed the door. Lizzie untied the stocking from the bedpost. She tried not to look at Sam's twisted, waxen face, his blackened tongue hanging loose from the corner of his mouth, but she had to look; she couldn't help herself.

'We'll have to try to lift him onto the bed.'

Robert nodded. He managed to slide his arms around Sam and together they heaved him up. They laid him on his side and covered him with a sheet.

'*Dona ei requiem. Dona ei requiem*,' they whispered. Lizzie hugged Robert.

'He was a good man,' Robert sobbed. 'This shouldn't have happened.'

Joan led Reverend Wallace into the kitchen. He had to duck to avoid bumping his head on the doorway. 'The children are at their aunt's house, in Fletcher Gate,' she said. 'I thought it best at the moment.' The vicar nodded. 'Very wise,' he said. He removed his hat and attempted to brush the rain from the crown.

Sam's body was laid out in its coffin, ready to be sealed and taken to the church. His face was still distorted and his neck bore black welts from the stocking.

'I should not allow an interment in the churchyard,' the

vicar said as he stared out the window, his view obscured by raindrops smattering against the glass. He glanced back at Joan. Her face was ashen, her eyes bruised through lack of sleep. She rested her hands on the edge of the coffin and gazed at Sam.

'However,' his cane gave a decisive tap on the floor, 'there is an area near the north door that is not consecrated. I have decided to permit the burial there.' Joan sighed with relief.

'Thank you' she whispered.

'You must be discreet, Mrs Elliott. There will be gossip and rumour.' Wallace drew out a handkerchief and blew his aquiline nose. 'I cannot deny that Samuel has committed a crime in the eyes of the Lord, however his crime was borne of deep sorrow and shame.' The vicar's voice was quiet, not the usual melodic sound Joan was used to hearing during one of his soporific sermons. 'I have grown used to seeing my parishioners growing thinner and my congregation dwindling. These are hard times indeed. We are all sinners in the eyes of God, but it is my Christian duty to show compassion and kindness to all God's people, even those who...take their own lives.' He gave an embarrassed smile. 'I shall make sure that the coffin is sealed before the service, and I shall also do my best to fend off the worst of the tittle-tattle, but the truth is bound to come out.'

Joan nodded.

'I have made my decision. I pray it is the right one. '

Lizzie drew her shawl around her and tucked her hands inside it. The wind stung her cheeks. Whirling leaves made a chaotic bid for freedom before being whipped back into the graveyard. Robert blew on his fingers and rubbed his hands together. 'Long enough service, isn't it?' he commented.

At that moment the church door opened and the parishioners filed out behind the coffin, which was held aloft by men from the workshop. Joan and her children walked at the head of the entourage. Robert and Lizzie joined them at the graveside.

'The Lord giveth and the Lord taketh away,' recited the vicar. Then the coffin was lowered. The vicar's words were carried upon the wind. 'Ashes to ashes, dust to dust...'

Caroline Elliott took a handful of earth and threw it into the grave. Her mother did the same. Michael rubbed his eyes. He looked around, half expecting his father to arrive at any moment. Lizzie and Robert said their Pater Noster along with the Lord's Prayer. Afterwards, the vicar shot them a disapproving glance as he noticed them crossing themselves. Finally, he moved away from the graveside along with a handful of more well-to-do people. Lizzie overheard a hushed conversation between the vicar and one of the women.

'I heard a rumour that it was a suicide. I'm surprised that you buried him in the churchyard.'

Reverend Wallace shook his head. 'No, no, natural causes apparently. His heart gave out. He was found in his bed.' The woman appeared to accept the explanation. 'Goodbye, Reverend. It was a very respectable service, given the circumstances.'

Lizzie returned to Robert's side. She tapped him on the shoulder.

'They don't know,' she whispered. 'The vicar must know what has happened, but no one else.'

Robert's expression was one of horror.

Lizzie continued, 'If the vicar had known the truth, surely he would have refused to bury Sam in the churchyard?' She looked around. Reverend Wallace was saying goodbye to the other members of the congregation.

Robert considered for a moment: 'Maybe he felt sorry for Joan and the children' he said.

Lizzie sighed. 'Either way, it's too late; it's done now.'

'But it's not too late for everyone else,' Robert said as he glanced round the churchyard. The men from the workshop had been joined by their wives and children.

The younger men stood with their hats in their hands, directionless and dejected.

'Mr Betts isn't here, is he?' observed Lizzie.

'No, he's not. Neither is Ben.'

'Where are they?'

'Visiting relatives in Ashfield; at least that's what I've been told.' Robert kicked at a mound of earth. 'Betts wouldn't dare show his face here today, not if he knows what's good for him. Everyone blames him for what's happened to Sam.' He sniffed. 'Question is, what do we do about it?'

Joan Elliott approached the twins. 'Thank you for coming today,' she murmured. 'It means a lot to me.' She fought back tears. Lizzie drew her hands from beneath her shawl and embraced Joan. The children clustered round them. Robert crouched down so that he was face to face with Michael.

'Be a good boy, won't you? Look after your mother. I know you're little, but you must grow up now. One day you'll be a man, and then you will understand.' He ruffled the little boy's hair. Rose took Michael's hand and led him back to the family.

As Robert stared at the gaunt faces of his fellow workers, Lizzie caught his eye. She understood his expression as if it had been her own. He was sad and angry at the same time. When he had that look on his face, she knew he was about to do something impetuous. True to form, Robert seized a poster that had been tied to the church railings. He climbed onto one of the tombs and addressed the crowd.

'What kind of country punishes its hardworking people? Yet again we suffer because of the actions of our so-called betters. Well they've got what they wanted, one less mouth to feed. Sam Elliott was a good man and a good friend. Now his children have no father. Are we expected to stand by while our fellow stockingers suffer? Should we not stand together?'

The men murmured agreement.

Robert recognised men who had been framebreaking earlier that year. 'We must be united. If we fight back, the punishment is to be sent to a colony in Australia. How long before it means the gallows?'

The crowd became more vocal. There were cries of anger and fear. On every face was an expression of terror.

'We should do everything in our power to show that we are not beaten.' Robert held the poster out in front of him, at arm's length: 'This is what I think of their wide frames and their law.'

Slowly he tore the poster in two from top to bottom. The crowd cheered.

'The hand is not one of a gentleman,' said the colonel as he examined the document. 'Look at the spelling, the grammar, the punctuation. This is not a person with an education.'

His lieutenant stepped closer to the desk and leaned over it. 'Could it be someone masquerading as an oaf? To put us off the scent?'

The colonel shook his head. 'I do not know, of course, but I would wager that this is someone with a grudge. Probably he has been put out of work.'

The lieutenant took up a magnifying glass and scrutinised the writing.

'This isn't the only one,' Musters said.

'No?'

'All the hosiers have received copies. They woke this morning to find the declarations pinned to their doors.'

'In the same hand?'

'No,' Colonel Musters said as he sat down, 'that's the bizarre thing. They all claim to be written by Ned Ludd, but the handwriting is different on all of them.' He leaned back in his seat. For a moment the crackling fire was the only sound. The Colonel placed his hands together in an arch.

'Do we know where the wider frames are?'

His lieutenant took up a sheaf of papers and nodded. 'I have a list of those workshops which have been attacked, and those which have not. We can assume this declaration indicates that the framebreakers will target all the workshops with wider frames.'

The colonel drew his breath slowly. 'So, all we have to do is discover the location of the unfortunate frame owner who is to be the next victim.'

The lieutenant held up a list. 'There are five in the city centre alone.'

Musters pondered if he could assemble a detachment of troops to guard every workshop.

'Is there any report from informants?'

'Very little: they are tight lipped.'

The colonel snorted, 'Honour among the criminal classes, I suppose.'

'Very probably,' said the lieutenant. 'However, there is one piece of news which may be significant.'

Musters fixed him in his gaze: 'Go on.'

'One of the frameworkers,' he reported as he searched the previous day's newspaper, 'Samuel Elliott, was found dead in his bed. Turns out he'd been laid off the day before, from the workshop of Mr Matthew Betts.'

'Are you thinking that there might be some sort of retribution?'

The lieutenant nodded. 'I believe it is highly likely. Apparently there was a disturbance at Elliott's funeral.'

'What kind of disturbance?' Musters frowned.

'Nothing that warranted arrest; but from what I gather, there was rabble rousing and possible incitement to framebreaking.'

The colonel's eyes flashed, 'Damn it man! We should have been present at the churchyard. The city's like a tinderbox. Anything can spark it off.' He stood and began to pace. 'If the common people believe, even mistakenly, that one of their own has died at the hands, albeit indirectly, at the hands of their betters, it could cause a revolt. We must do everything in our power to quell it.'

He took a decanter from a cabinet and poured himself a large glass of brandy. He gulped it down, then croaked, 'Where precisely is this Betts workshop?'

'Tough side of beef, that.' Mr Betts mopped his gravy with a slice of bread.

Ben pushed his plate away: 'I've had enough.'

'There's nothing wrong with the potatoes, lad.' He gave his nephew a disapproving glance. Ben sighed. He finished his cup of tea. He caught his mother's eye.

'Aren't you hungry?'

Ben shook his head. 'No mother.'

Mrs Harwood grimaced. 'You should be grateful we have enough to eat. There are plenty of people who would be glad for that food. Even if the beef is a little—'

'Give it to them, then.' Ben folded his arms.

'Don't speak to your mother like that!' Matthew Betts looked at his sister. She fixed her expression and resumed eating. Betts frowned. 'Benjamin, apologise at once.'

Ben avoided making eye contact with his uncle.

'You're almost of age, boy, but that does not mean you are too old for a thrashing.'

Ben stood, his chair scraping the floor. He glared at his mother. 'How can you let him threaten me like that? He's not my father.' He threw his napkin down and stamped out, slamming the door behind him. Mr Betts shook his head.

'He's beyond control; he needs to be taught a lesson.'

Mrs Harwood gently touched her brother's arm. 'No, Matthew. Let him go. It'll blow over. He's like his father. He flares up quickly, but he'll soon calm if left alone.'

'*In nomine patri, et fili et spiritu sancti. Amen.*'

Père Bertrand made the sign of the cross and brought the service to a close. Lizzie opened her eyes. The chapel was almost empty. She remained kneeling for a while, her eyes now fixed on the statue of the madonna. She thought of Joan Elliott and her children, who now had no father. She got up and sat back on the bench, drawing her shawl around her shoulders in preparation for her walk home.

'Where is your brother this evening?'

Père Bertrand stood at the end of the pew. Lizzie cast her eyes downwards.

'I honestly don't know, father.' She sighed and met his gaze.

'I hope he is not drinking and gambling and—' The priest broke off and nodded towards the statue of St Mary Magdalene. Then he began polishing his glasses on his robe. 'I expect the *coquin* will come for confession tomorrow?'

Lizzie gave a knowing smile: 'I expect so.'

The priest wished her *bon soir* and left. Lizzie stood. Noticing that someone had left the day's newspaper on one of the pews, she picked it up and walked over to the statue of the female saint; the only woman with her breasts brazenly exposed in a chapel.

'I really hope Robert's not going to get into trouble,' she whispered. 'If you can mend your ways, anyone can.'

'Sarah will be sorry she's missed you,' said Emma as she poured Robert's ale.

'Me?' He raised his eyebrows.

'Yes you!' Emma smiled. 'She said something about giving you your winnings.'

'That was ages ago,' said Robert.

'Well, she never forgets.' Emma leaned over to him and said, 'Between you and me, I think she's quite sweet on you.'

The ale house clock chimed seven. Two men entered. Robert instantly recognised them from Sam's funeral. One of them briefly held his right hand over his eye. Robert noticed a man near the fireside respond by holding his left hand over his eye, mirroring the gesture. A secret greeting.

They bought drinks and joined their fellow Luddite near the fire. Robert downed the remains of his ale and walked over to them. One of the men stood and patted him on the back.

'This lad gave a fine speech at Sam Elliott's funeral. Tore the bill in half, he did.'

The older man smiled. 'Are you as brave in your actions as you are in your words, lad?' he asked.

Robert nodded, 'I want to see justice done.'

'As we all do!' He put out his hand: 'Peter Connor.'

Robert shook his hand, 'Robert Molyneux.' He frowned a little: 'You are not a stockinger, are you?'

Connor chuckled. 'No, I'm not. How can you tell?'

'You are too well fed for a start. Your hands are too rough as well.'

Connor examined his palms and fingers, calloused from handling the reins of the coach.'I drive a gentleman's carriage,' he said.

One of the other men leant closer to Robert and lowered his voice: 'This must remain secret, you understand?'

Robert nodded. 'Would your master not approve?'

Connor smiled. 'On the contrary, I know that he would. He's unusual to say the least. More importantly, he has no need of me tonight.'

At that moment the tavern door flew open and Ben Harwood strode in. He slapped his coins on the bar.

'Someone's in a foul mood.' Emma addressed him.

'Just give me a pint.'

'Let me guess,' Emma said as she poured his ale, 'you've been at loggerheads with your uncle again.'

Ben nodded. The landlady handed him the tankard. He drank half of it in a matter of seconds.

'Steady on,' Emma warned him. 'Pace yourself.'

Ben wiped his mouth with his hand. 'Where's Sarah?' he growled.

'She's gone out,' Emma answered as she poured herself

a measure of brandy.

'Out?' Ben sounded incredulous.

'I think she might have gone to church.'

Ben choked on his beer: 'You're joking.'

Emma shook her head. 'She's been behaving a bit odd of late. Very picky about her customers.' Emma's eyes met Ben's: 'She said she was fed up with men taking more than they'd paid for.'

'Magotty bitch,' Ben snarled as he finished his ale. Noticing Robert, he said, 'You didn't tell me Robert was here.'

Emma glanced over at the men near the fire. 'I thought he'd gone.'

Ben walked over to them. 'Is this a private gathering?' he asked.

'Ben!' Robert stood up and introduced the others: 'Peter Connor, Joe Sawyer, and you know Stephen Hodgkinson, from the workshop.'

'Ben's uncle owns the workshop,' Stephen explained.

Connor looked concerned.

'Don't worry,' Ben said, 'there's no love lost between us. I'm as sick of him as everyone else.'

'That's good,' Connor remarked. 'The less you care about the frame owners, the easier it is to break the frames.' He put down his empty tankard: 'Now, gentlemen,' he said as he took out his pocket watch, 'we'll go to join the others. Eight o'clock at Hollow Stone.'

Lizzie poured herself a cup of tea. It was nearly two hours since she had returned home from the chapel. She expected Robert to walk in at any moment. He had been later than this before, especially if he had been gambling.

There was a pile of mending next to the frame. Lizzie extracted one of Robert's shirts. Threading the needle, she assessed a tear in the sleeve, and the cuffs needed darning again too. Perhaps she could sew a small piece of fabric along the edge of each cuff to protect it. Small neat stitches appeared along the material. Lizzie had performed this task countless times. Maybe one day she would darn her husband's sleeves. It would probably be somewhat like living with her brother, but, she hoped, less worrying. What sort of man would she consider marrying? She had never had a proposal. There had been a pleasant-looking young man who used to smile at her in the chapel, he had curly red hair and ice blue eyes, but his family had moved away and she never saw him again. If she did marry, what would her children be like? Somehow Lizzie could not imagine having a large family like Joan's; you'd need eyes in the back of your head. Biting off the cotton, she inspected her work. She folded the shirt and placed it on Robert's bed.

Returning to the kitchen, she took up the newspaper. Samuel Elliott's funeral was reported as was the latest framebreaking. Someone calling himself Ned Ludd had written a declaration to the frame owners saying that he would only break the wide frames that were putting men out of work. Lizzie yawned. She caught sight of her father's portrait on the mantlepiece.

'Papa,' she said, 'you never thought we should see such trouble here. What would you do?'

The picture was silent.

'Is everyone ready?' Connor pulled his kerchief over his nose; the other men did likewise. Brandishing hammers and axes, they swore their loyalty. Joe Sawyer held up two pistols; Connor did the same. They set their weapons at half-cock and concealed them inside their jackets.

In silence they made their way up towards Trivett Square. The pale moon observed them as they broke the locked door of the workshop. They ascended the stairs.

'The wider frames are at the far end,' someone called. Ben's eyes shone with excitement.

'Guard the door,' Connor ordered, and Joe Sawyer remained near the entrance, his pistols at the ready.

'I must have left the blasted thing in the workshop.' Matthew Betts turned over papers and rummaged through a drawer in his desk, searching for the ledger. He glanced at the clock. It was quarter to nine, well before the curfew. He clicked his tongue: 'No, it can't wait until tomorrow.' He picked up his hat, took the workshop key from his desk and left the house.

Joe aimed his gun at the man who had appeared in the yard. 'Stay back or I'll shoot.'

'What the devil do you mean, man? This is *my* workshop.'

'I'm warning you, stay where you are.'

'Is that what you are? Luddite?'

Betts looked up at the window of the workshop. He could hear the clatter of destruction. A pane of glass shattered and part of a frame flew out.

'What in God's name are they doing?'

'I thought that was obvious,' Joe sneered as he cocked his pistol.

Suddenly, the sound of horses hooves approaching took Joe's attention and he turned away from Betts who was frozen to the spot in the yard.

'It's the militia!' he shouted up the stairs. 'Everyone, get out!'

A group of soldiers jogged into the yard and took position. Betts found himself caught between them and the workshop. He dashed inside the doorway.

'On my command,' Musters shouted, 'shoot on sight!'

Connor looked out of the workshop window. 'We're stranded,' he said. 'Joe and I will fire on them, and the rest of you can make a break for it. Every man for himself!'

Mr Betts cowered in the downstairs office, as Joe sidled up to the doorway and fired a shot at the soldiers. They fired back. A bullet hit a lead drainpipe near the door and ricocheted, ringing like an out of tune bell. Another pierced a hole in the window pane. While they were re-loading, he made a run for the gate. Musters turned his horse and took aim. He fired. The pistol cracked and Joe collapsed on the ground, dropping his second pistol. Robert saw what had happened from the window.

'Joe's been shot!' he cried. 'Oh God, is he dead?'

'I expect so, lad.' Connor realised the young man had never seen anything like it. 'Come with me; I'll cover you while they reload.'

The other men ran down the stairs and scattered across the yard. Connor remained in the doorway.

'Give me one of your pistols,' Ben called.

Sensing the lad was unafraid, he did so: 'Pull that lever back until it clicks, then it's cocked. Fire when you're ready.'

Connor leapt from the workshop door and concealed himself next to an outhouse. The soldiers fired once again. Brick dust flew out where a bullet hit the wall next to him. He flattened himself against the side door, then ran to the back of the building and heaved himself over the wall.

'I'm getting too old for this sort of lark,' he gasped, before rushing headlong down the hill to where his horse was tethered.

Ben waited near the door as the others escaped. Robert joined him.

'Ben, that man's dead.'

'I know,' Ben snarled. 'Bastards!' he shouted.

Mr Betts recognised his nephew's voice. 'Ben?'

The young man hadn't noticed his uncle who was crouched in a corner of the office. Ben turned and aimed the pistol at him.

'What are you doing?' Robert hissed, his eyes widening.

'Going to give me a thrashing now, are you?' Ben said. His eyes narrowed.

Matthew Betts held his hands up in front of him. 'No, please,' he begged, 'let me go.'

Ben shook his head, 'You've given me your last beating, and you've seen your last dawn.'

Robert seized Ben's arm, 'No!' he cried.

'Leave go Frenchman!' Ben shouted, 'or I'll shoot you instead!'

For a moment the two lads struggled. As they fought, the pistol fired. Betts slumped against the wall. Immediately, Ben fled. Following Connor's stratagem, he darted behind the outhouse and clambered over the wall. He tore his kerchief from his face and shoved it into his pocket.

Robert stood frozen in the office, his posture unsteady and his jaws clenched. He dropped to his knees. Colonel Musters planted his hand firmly upon Robert's shoulder: 'I arrest you in the name of His Majesty the King.'

Two of the soldiers then hauled Robert to his feet and dragged him into the yard. Tears were pricking at his eyes.

'Murderer!' one of the soldiers spat. 'Where's Ned Ludd now, eh?'

Ben silently entered his uncle's house. A lamp was still burning in the study. He picked it up and ascended the stairs.

'Matthew?' Ben's mother appeared in the doorway of her bedroom.

'No, mother, it's me.'

'Oh, Ben,' she said as she rubbed her eyes, 'I was asleep. Where is your uncle?'

Ben shrugged. 'I have no idea. I've only just got back from the Angel. I've not seen him.'

Mrs Harwood frowned. 'He's probably had to go to the workshop for something. He did mention he couldn't find the wages ledger.'

'He should have left it until tomorrow.' Ben's voice showed no emotion.

'Well, goodnight then,' his mother said and kissed him on the cheek.

'Goodnight, Mama.'

Ben entered his bedroom and closed the door.

Bare beech branches reached toward the silent sky as the grey dawn ushered in a fog that shrouded the town. A funereal chorus of crows jeered at Thomas Jackson as he approached Trivett Square. He was greeted there by a young soldier, his red coat a shock of colour through the mist.

'What's cracked off here?' Jackson stepped towards the workshop. The sentry lifted up his rifle.

'You may not enter, sir.'

'What do you mean, lad? Where is Mr Betts?'

The soldier rested his rifle on his shoulder; the older man appeared to be no threat.

'There was another episode of framebreaking last night. The owner of the workshop was killed.'

Jackson took a step back. 'Killed?'

The sentry nodded, 'Shot by one of the so-called Luddites. He has been taken to the gaol.'

'Does Katherine know? She's Mr Betts' sister. And what about his nephew, Ben. They're his only family.'

'They have been informed.'

Jackson shook his head. 'I can't believe he's dead.' He drew out his handkerchief and blew his nose. 'Do you know who killed him?'

'I was there when we caught him. He gave his name as Robert Molyneux.'

Jackson's normally ruddy face lost its colour. 'You must have the wrong man. Granted, he's lively, a bit fiery at times, but he's not a murderer.'

'We arrested him in the workshop. He had a pistol.'

'Dear God!' Jackson was shaken.

'He was the only person left in the room, apart from Mr Betts.'

'What was he doing with a pistol? He's a stocking knitter.'

'You tell me,' the sentry sniffed. 'It was an old one though—a French model.'

'Bloody hell!'

'Do you know Molyneux well, sir?'

'Apparently not as well as I thought I did.'

The sentry fixed Jackson in his gaze: 'Do you have any idea who his accomplices might be?'

Jackson shook his head. 'Why these men want to destroy their frames, their livelihood, makes no sense to me,' he sighed. 'There has been trouble recently though. Betts had to lay off some of them, but he had no choice. You can't keep men on the payroll if there's not enough work.'

Understanding that Jackson was not involved the soldier nodded. 'You had better inform the rest of the workers that the workshop is closed. Make sure they know the reason, and that there will be serious consequences for framebreaking.'

Jackson hummed his agreement. 'I best tell Lizzie as well.'

'Who?'

'Molyneux's sister. She works at home. She probably knows nothing about this.'

Lizzie pulled on her boots and drew her shawl around her shoulders. Robert had never stayed out all night before. 'Something's wrong,' she said to her father's portrait, 'I know it.' She was just about to leave when there was a rap on the door. She caught her breath and lifted the latch to find Thomas Jackson standing outside.

'Oh, Mr Jackson, I was just about to go out.'

'To look for Robert?' He entered the kitchen.

She nodded. 'How did you know?'

'You'd better sit down, Liz.'

'Please don't tell me he's dead.' She crossed herself.

'No, he's alive. But he's in trouble.'

'What kind of trouble?'

'He was arrested last night—framebreaking.'

Lizzie sighed and closed her eyes.

'But that's not the worst of it,' said Jackson.

'What has happened?'

'Robert shot Mr Betts; he's dead.'

Lizzie exhaled sharply, 'Robert? He shot...'

Jackson nodded. 'The soldiers caught him red-handed. He had a pistol.'

Lizzie was dumbfounded. The silence was broken by St Mary's chiming eight o'clock. Lizzie rested her head on her hands. 'We do not own a pistol. And Robert wouldn't know how to fire one.'

'Well, he did last night.'

'Where is he?'

'In the gaol.'

'I must go to see him. I'll find out what really happened.' She stood. 'Will I be allowed to see him?'

Jackson shook his head, 'I don't know, Liz.'

She glanced at her own stocking frame. Jackson followed her gaze. He sniffed.

'Considering the circumstances, I shan't expect a day's work from you today. But I'll have to knock tuppence off your wages.'

Lizzie nodded. Though she had to see Robert—she would know instantly if he was to blame. 'Very well, Mr Jackson. Now, I really must go.'

She showed him out and ran towards the gaol.

The guard pushed open Robert's cell door. 'You've got a visitor.' He showed Lizzie inside: 'Ten minutes, no longer,' he snapped.

Lizzie nodded as Robert leapt up and threw his arms around her. 'Lizzie, I thought I would never see you again,' he sobbed.

Lizzie stroked Robert's shoulders, trying to calm him. 'Tell me what happened.'

He sat on the bench where he had spent a sleepless

night.

'Mr Betts—'

'I know. Mr Jackson told me.' She lowered her voice: 'What were you doing with a pistol?'

'We only meant to break the wide frames. But then the soldiers fired on us. Joe Sawyer was shot. Everyone else got away except Ben and me.'

'Ben was there?'

Robert nodded. 'He had the pistol; he was going to fire at the soldiers. But then he realized that his uncle was in the workshop.'

'What was he doing in there at night?'

'I don't know. He wasn't there when we went in, I'm certain of it. We had to break down the door.' Robert closed his eyes, remembering. 'Ben pointed the pistol at Mr Betts. I tried to take it from him, then it fired.'

'Who fired it?'

'I don't know. It just went off. I didn't mean to kill him. I was trying to stop Ben.'

'Ben got away?'

Robert nodded, 'He ran out; somehow he escaped.'

'Why don't you tell them the truth? Surely it was Ben who was to blame?'

Robert shook his head, 'It's not that simple. We were both holding the gun when it fired.'

'But it was an accident?'

'It was no accident that we were framebreaking,' Robert hissed. 'Mr Betts treated Ben shamefully. He was always thrashing him. Making him look stupid, humiliating him.'

'But he didn't deserve to die.'

'No, he didn't.' Robert's eyes were red. 'But if I inform on Ben, he'll hang for certain.'

'Why should you suffer on his behalf?' Lizzie took hold of him once more: 'They'll hang you, won't they?'

Robert's dark eyes met Lizzie's: 'Not while they know I've got information.'

Lizzie frowned: 'What do you mean?'

'They know that I'm more use to them alive. I know who the other framebreakers are.'

'But they will torture you to make you tell. That's what happens to prisoners if they think you know something.'

Robert ran his hands through his hair. 'When the Bastille fell, there were people who had been in there for years without a trial. Perhaps it will be the same here.' He looked into her eyes: 'I truly believe we are on the brink of revolution, Lizzie.'

'This is madness,' she whispered. 'There isn't going to be a revolution in this country. No one is going to storm Nottingham gaol.'

'You don't know that.'

Lizzie bit her lip. 'The sentence for framebreaking is transportation, but for murder it's the gallows. We have got to find a way to absolve you of killing Mr Betts.'

At that moment the cell door scraped open.

'You must go now, Miss,' the guard barked. 'You've had your ten minutes.'

Lizzie kissed Robert's cheek. 'I will think of something,' she promised.

Robert watched as the guard ushered her out and locked the door.

The afternoon sun had forced its way out of the fog and now slanted through the deserted chapel windows, its golden shafts illuminating the sparkling particles of dust and highlighting the cracks in the plaster statues of saints. Lizzie silently closed the door as she entered. She crossed herself and gazed around the pews, making sure that there was no one there to hear her. She approached the icon of the Virgin Mary. The Madonna's robe was glowing azure blue in the dying light. Lizzie drew out her rosary and knelt.

'Dear mother,' she whispered. 'what must I do? I do not believe that Robert is capable of killing someone. He did not intend any harm.' Lizzie sighed, 'That is not quite true. He intended to break the frames, but only because Sam was put out of work. I know Sam took his own life, and I know that is the deepest sin, but I truly believe that he was a good man and did not deserve to suffer. Now his children have no father. And now Robert faces harsh judgment for something he did not do. Please, mother, will you hear my prayer? Even if we do not deserve a miracle, please, show me the way.' She raised her eyes to the fixed, gentle expression on the statue's face. 'Give me a sign. I implore you.'

Lizzie closed her eyes once more. She heard a sound behind her. She jumped up and saw Père Bertrand standing close to the front pew. He motioned his hands downwards and brought them together in front of him.

'*Doucement*, Lizette. I do not mean to startle you.' His voice was kind. 'Would you like me to say prayers for you? You look troubled. What is the matter?'

Lizzie knew she should tell him. The priest must know her thoughts, and what had happened to Robert. To conceal anything would be sinful.

'It's Robert,' she began. 'I am afraid he is in serious trouble.'

The priest polished his spectacles on his robe. He replaced them and latticed his fingers in front of his rotund middle. 'What is it this time? Gambling? Drinking? Or women?' He peered at her over his glasses.

Lizzie sighed, 'I'm afraid it's much worse than that; he's in prison.'

Père Bertrand took a deep breath. He crossed himself. 'Why is he in there?'

Lizzie glanced to one side. Where should she begin?

'A friend of his at work lost his employment. The machinery is changing, and not for the better; every time they replace the frames with the wider ones, a lot of men lose their work.' She looked at the priest and wondered if it made any sense to him at all. 'Finally, they decided to—to smash the machines that were putting them out of work.

Last night, during the framebreaking, the frame owner was shot.' She felt tears coming to her eyes. 'Robert was found with the pistol—'

'He had a gun? *Mon Dieu*!' Père Bertrand clapped his hand to his mouth when he realised what he had just said. He crossed himself and muttered a hasty apology for his blasphemy.

'It did not belong to Robert. I am convinced that Robert did not deliberately kill Mr Betts.'

The priest sank onto the pew. Lizzie joined him. She was silent for a moment. She turned to face him. 'Father, if you could talk to him... Hear his confession...'

'Robert must be ready to confess his sins. He must want to repent. Does he?'

Lizzie feared he would not.

The priest shook his head. 'I hope this trouble will not turn into a revolution. When that happened in France, the angry men smashed the windows of my chapel in Paris. They pulled down the saints and stole the chalice. I had to flee.'

Lizzie noticed the sadness in his eyes. He had never spoken of this before now.

'I escaped when a kind family took me in. They pretended that I was their uncle and I was smuggled to England by a merchant. He was importing brandy of all things.' Père Bertrand gave a faint smile. 'I do not think I can help you, Lizette. It is in your brother's hands to choose the right path. He must want to repent. I shall pray to Saint Anthony for his carnal sins, and to *La Madeleine*. But for his involvement in what appears to be the beginnings of sedition,' he sighed, 'only God knows what will happen.'

'God would not want an innocent man to suffer, surely?'

'Many innocents suffer in this world. It is not for you to question the divine plan of God.' He stood. 'I must go now to prepare for vespers. Keep praying to the Virgin.'

He patted her on the shoulder and made his way to the vestry.

Lizzie looked at the statue of the Virgin. If only her own mother or father were here. Papa would know what to do, surely. She felt her shoulders drop. Lizzie drew her shawl around her and left the chapel.

A bitter breeze lashed her cheeks as she dawdled down the street. St Mary's chimed four o'clock. The sun was already setting, sending a crown of gold into the sky. Leaves whirled in tormented circles, forced up by the wind. Lost in her thoughts, she gradually became aware of the sound of children's voices at the corner of Bellar Gate. As she turned into the road, she noticed a group of them playing. One of the little boys looked up, forgot his hopscotch and ran over to her. 'Lizzie! It's Lizzie!' Michael Elliott threw his arms around her and hugged her.

'Steady Michael, you'll knock me over.' His cheeks were glowing from the chilly air. Lizzie took hold of his little hands. 'You should go home; it's getting dark now, and you don't want to be out in the cold.'

'If I get ill, you can cure me again. I've been telling the other boys about how you made me better.'

'Have you?' Lizzie frowned a little.

'Yes. You gave me a special drink and sang a magic song to me. Are you a witch?'

'Why ever would you say that?'

'One of them said you are. He said his mama saw you in the graveyard. Were you making spells and talking to ghosts?'

'She's the French witch!' one of the boys shouted.

'French witch!' the others repeated.

Lizzie shook her head. 'I'm not, Michael. You mustn't believe them.'

Michael frowned. He looked at the boys then turned back to Lizzie. 'Do you know where my papa's gone?'

'He's gone to heaven.' Lizzie sighed. Père Bertrand

would no doubt disagree with her.

'That's what mama says.'

'Well, she's right.'

A stone caught Lizzie on the elbow. She looked over at the group of boys. They were only a couple of years older than Michael and already they had decided she was to be hated. Another stone was hurled and caught Michael on the shoulder. He picked it up and threw it back.

'Stop it!' he shouted. 'It hurts.'

The other boys began to pelt Lizzie and Michael with pebbles, chanting 'French witch!' Lizzie grabbed Michael's hand and ran. She could feel tears in her eyes, but she would not show her fear to the little boy. They reached the Elliotts' house. Lizzie hammered on the door.

'Lizzie! I wasn't expecting you.' Joan noticed fear in Lizzie's eyes. 'What's the matter?' she asked.

The group of lads arrived at the corner of Barker Gate and continued their chanting: 'French witch! French witch!' They picked up small stones and threw them.

Joan was furious. 'Get inside, quickly!' She ushered Lizzie and Michael indoors then stormed down the street towards the children.

'Little beggars!' She cuffed the eldest lad and he howled. 'Off with you now!' Joan shouted, 'or I'll knock you into next week. I know all your mothers. Go home before I tell them what little devils you are.' The boys panicked and started to run. She picked up a stone and threw it at them. It caught one of them on the ankle and he squealed.

Joan watched them go then she returned to her house. Lizzie was sitting inside with Michael on her knee. Joan closed the door and began to make tea for them.

'Little demons,' she grimaced as she filled the pot, 'you know how people gossip.' She poked the fire and returned to the table.

'And you!' She picked Michael up and sat him near the fire: 'What have I told you about telling people all your business? Do you remember what I said?'

Michael shook his head and said, 'I'm sorry, Mama.'

Joan sat next to Lizzie and began to pour the tea.

'Thanks for bringing him home,' she said. 'The girls should be back from the market soon. One of the stall holders has been giving us any unsold vegetables lately, if they go late enough. If you like, you can have some. They usually get quite a bit.' She noticed Lizzie's expression. Lizzie rubbed her eyes and tried not to sob. How could such young children be so cruel? Joan stroked her arm.

'They'll not do it again. Any more bother and I'll go round to their houses and have it out with their parents. Then they'll be sorry.'

'No, Joan, please don't. I don't want them to turn against you as well, for defending me.'

Joan passed a tea cup to Michael, who held it with both hands and gazed into the fire.

'Robert's in trouble.' Lizzie said.

'I heard. Is it true that he's in the gaol?'

Lizzie nodded: 'They think he killed Mr Betts.'

Joan sipped her tea. 'And what do you think?'

'I don't think he's capable of it. He said it was an accident. He's always been in the wrong place at the wrong time.' Lizzie looked at Michael. She remembered what Robert was like at the same age, always getting into trouble, always coming home with torn clothes, wearing out his shoes.

'Papa used to say he was a *vilain*,' she said as she looked back to Joan. 'He can be reckless, but he's not a murderer.'

'Bad business, m'lord.' Connor sipped his beer and visibly slumped in the fireside chair. The young man seated opposite him leaned closer.

'You mustn't call me that,' he whispered. 'Please address me as Mr Gordon.'

Connor glanced around the tavern, nervous that someone had heard his mistake. The other customers in the Angel were drinking and talking amongst themselves. Satisfied that no one had taken any notice, he drew his breath deeply. 'Sorry, Mr Gordon.'

'No harm done.'

'What I was saying, though, was that the last raid was chaos,' he muttered. 'There were a lot of us, but the militia meant business. They weren't going back empty handed.'

'How many were arrested?'

'Five or six. They weren't the worst off, though.'

The younger man gulped his beer, his eyes wanting explanation.

'At least two of them ended up dead. Along with the frame owner.'

'Good God!' His pale face blanched almost white. 'Were they shot?'

Connor nodded. 'They're young lads, mostly; younger than yourself, some of them. They're brave, but they can be foolish. The older ones aren't much better. They take too many risks.' Connor rubbed his brow.

The young man nodded, chewing his fingernail.

'I know you've not wanted to get involved until now, sir, but I really think they'd listen to you.' Connor finished his ale. They were silent for a moment.

'You are right. I cannot stand by and do nothing. Not now that they are risking their lives,' the young man determined. 'What about their families?'

'They're starving. Every man in work on the wider frames means six out of it. Mr Gordon: you're educated, you're well bred, more importantly you're a natural leader.'

The young man's face flushed slightly with pride. He paused for a moment, considering what might be done. Suddenly they were interrupted.

'Penny for them, sir?' The girl collected their empty tankards and gave a seductive smile to the handsome young gentleman. Blinking his silver-blue eyes, he reciprocated her sensual expression.

'My thoughts are, I believe, worth a little more than

that.'

'Maybe after you've finished here, you'd like to share some of them with me? It won't cost you more than two shillings.'

Connor sniffed his disapproval. Undeterred, the girl toyed with a lock of her light auburn hair.

'A nice young gentleman such as you, I'd do something special for you. Just come to me later.' She winked at him and made her way back to the bar.

Connor took out his pocket watch. 'Five o'clock,' he said.

'Almost time for dinner,' the younger man said, smiling. 'Go along and wait for me. I'll be there soon, don't worry. And I will seriously consider all that you've said.'

Connor stood and turned to his master. 'What do you plan to do?' he asked.

'I'm going to spend two shillings.'

'Here we are, sir.' The girl looked back at him and noticed how he limped as he ascended the stairs. She led him into her room. It was dark, yet cozy; infused with the faint scent of sweat mixed with lavender.

'What is your name, my cherub?' he asked.

She lit a candle, its light revealing a bed large enough for two.

'Do cherubs have names?'

'Not strictly, but angels do.' He hung his fine worsted coat over a chair: 'Michael, Raphael,' he recited as he untied his silk cravat. 'Umbriel, Lucifer—'

'I've heard of him,' the girl giggled. 'Surely he's a devil?' She sat on her bed.

'Technically, a *fallen* angel.'

'Fallen angel, that's me,' she said, smiling. She pulled off her boots and began to unlace her dress: 'My name's Sarah.'

'Mr Gordon.'

They shook hands in a rather formal fashion, as though

they were being introduced at a society gathering.

'You're much better spoken than most of the Angel's customers, Mr Gordon. You don't sound local.'

'I'm not really. I was brought up in Aberdeen.'

'In Scotland?'

He nodded. 'My mother was Scottish.'

'You don't sound Scottish...'

'I was schooled at Harrow.'

'Ah!' Sarah smiled in a way that showed that this didn't really explain anything to her. She watched as he sat down and removed his boots; it seemed to cause him some discomfort. The reason he limped became clear and Sarah tried not to stare at his deformed foot. Instead she helped him remove his shirt, and then she unbuttoned his breeches. 'Oh, my goodness!' Sarah grinned.

Connor untethered the horses and climbed into the driver's seat of the coach. One of the horses gave a soft whinny, its breath cloudy in the cold air. St Mary's chimed quarter past. Connor hugged himself to keep warm. From his perch he could see right up Barker Gate and along Bellar Gate. Workers were making their way home, hurrying through the frosty streets. Many of them would be going home to empty bellies. Connor looked forward to being back at Newstead and tucking into his supper. He was glad for his thick gloves and woollen scarf. He wondered if his lordship would mind if he waited inside the coach, rather than outside. Maybe he should have stayed in the tavern.

'What a saucy trollop that girl was,' he mumbled to himself. However, she'd be warm and soft. His master was in the better place.

'Do you mean to bugger me, sir?' Sarah looked over her shoulder as Mr Gordon guided her onto her hands and knees on the bed. She did not sound alarmed, merely asking for information.

'Certainly not!' Her customer slid his hand over her belly and down. He began to stroke between her legs.

'I don't mind, you know,' she smiled.

'Really? Even though sodomy is a sin, not to mention against the law?'

She chuckled. '*Everything* I do is a sin. And if we did do it, well, I won't tell if you won't. Besides, I quite like it.'

He pondered her confession for a moment. 'Maybe another time. No, this...' he slid into her from behind...'is perfect for now.' Their breath steamed the window and the candle flickered as their initially languorous rhythm increased. Sarah moaned loudly in genuine pleasure:

'Mr Gordon! God you're good at it!'

He gripped her hips: 'You're uncommonly sensual,' he gasped. 'You could make a man spend just by looking at him.' He leaned forward and kissed the back of her neck. A moment later they dropped onto the bed.

'I do believe, Mr Gordon,' Sarah chuckled, 'that *that* was the best fuck I've ever had.' She sounded totally sincere. He laughed and stroked his gentle fingers over her cupid lips.

'Do you know how to do *La Gamuche*?' he asked.

'Is it a dance? I'm no dancer.'

'Neither am I. No, my dear, it's pleasuring a man with your mouth.'

'I've never heard it called that before. Why?'

'I would like you to do it for me. Would you be willing, or would it offend you?'

'Offend me? Of course not. Such a polite, clean gentleman as you, I'd gladly do it.'

'Would you do it now?' He smiled.

Sarah looked down in disbelief. 'Are you ready to go again?'

He nodded. She licked her lips.

Connor had a sudden feeling of falling, dropping from a high tower into space. He jolted awake. He was still seated on the coach. The horses were patiently standing before him. He drew out his watch: six o'clock. He climbed down from the seat and opened the monogrammed door nearest the pavement. The coach was empty. Obviously, his master was still in the tavern.

'Lord Byron's a slave to his animal appetites, isn't he?' Connor patted one of the horses. 'He's a decent sort, though. He's got a good heart.'

The horse nodded, the reins jingling. Connor chuckled.

'Have you had enough now?' Sarah panted, wrapping her arms around her apparently insatiable customer, 'because, Mr Gordon,' she laughed, 'I don't think I can keep up with you!'

He wiped the sweat from his brow and withdrew.

'Thank you, Sarah,' he sighed. 'I am fully satisfied.' He relaxed onto the pillows and stroked her hair. She noticed that he now had a rather troubled expression.

'What's the matter, sir? If you don't mind me asking...'

'I am a selfish brute.'

'No, definitely not!' Sarah contradicted him. 'I've known selfish men, and believe me, you are nothing like them.'

'Well, maybe not in bed, but generally I am. I've been wasting my time writing verses—'

'You write poems?' Sarah was impressed. 'You're an unusual man in lots of ways...'

'There are more important things than poetry. Only today I learnt that some of the frame breakers had been arrested and at least two of them killed.'

Sarah rested her head upon her hand: 'I know. One of them that's in gaol is Robert Molyneux. He lives down the road. And some of the soldiers had the nerve to come in here, all bragging and swilling—said their colonel had given them extra rations for being so efficient.'

'What colonel?'

'Musters they said his name was.'

An expression of recognition crossed the young man's face. He gave a hollow laugh. 'That blackguard married my childhood sweetheart.'

'Did he really sir?'

He got up and began to dress. 'Mary Chaworth. She'll regret that,' he sneered.

Sarah looked up at him: 'I reckon she'll regret not marrying *you*.' She reached out and stroked the front of his breeches. He looked down at her, his expression an odd mixture of pride and sadness.

'She once called me a lame brat.'

Sarah was horrified. She stood up. 'How cruel! You can't help the way you're made.' He pulled on his boots. Sarah stroked his shoulder, 'You may be cursed with a crippled foot, but you're blessed in other ways.'

He smiled and drew out a handful of coins.

'That's far more than two shillings, Mr Gordon.'

'I know. But you have given me far more than two shillings' worth of enjoyment, and a good deal of useful information.' He kissed her hand and then placed the coins in her palm.

'I'm glad to have served you so well.' She gave him a peck on the cheek. He pulled on his jacket.

'Now I really must go. Poor Mr Connor has been waiting for me like the faithful Leporello, frozen to the marrow on the fringe of the frosty fields.'

Sarah smiled at his turn of phrase, 'Who is Mr Connor?' she asked.

He replied without thinking, 'He's my coach driver.'

'Then you are a *real* gentleman, sir.'

He bit his lip. 'I am, but you must keep it secret.'

Sarah nodded. 'You can trust me,' she said.

'Can I?' His eyes met hers, 'Yes, I believe I can.'

Lizzie made her way down Stoney Street and turned into Barker Gate. It was dark, and she was acutely aware of the sound of her own footsteps. The sooner she was home and preparing a stew from the parsnips she had in her basket, the better. A small animal scuttled across her path. She gasped, and then sighed with relief. It was only a rat, not a ferocious dog. It scurried away down an alley and she was alone once more. The only light came from the ale house on the corner of the street. She could hear voices murmuring inside but was unable to pick out any distinct words. She could smell the scent of tobacco and stale beer as she passed. A few yards further on, Lizzie turned around. She thought she saw a shadowy figure leave the inn. She squinted in the dark, but could see no one. As she continued along the street, a cold knot of fear grew in her empty stomach. Was she being followed? Only a few hundred yards from home she quickened her pace.

'Don't cry out!' The man's voice was a gentle whisper. He pulled her into a doorway, his hand over her mouth. Lizzie struggled, but he held her tight: 'Do not be afraid. I won't hurt you.'

'Why should I believe you?' Lizzie gasped as he released her. She turned to face him. He was dark haired with pale skin. The collar of his long coat was pulled up; a black silk scarf covered his mouth and nose.

He took her hand: 'I am a gentleman, and I would not benefit from harming you.'

'What do you want?' Lizzie asked.

'Only to tell you that a stranger has your interests at heart...'

'What do you mean?'

'Captain Ludd is watching over you.'

'Who is he?' Lizzie had heard the name but was unsure that he was a real person.

'One who loves Liberty. A man who will not stand by and watch his fellow countrymen be beaten and starved into submission by a despotic government. It is a disgrace.' His eyes glowed with passion. 'I have been to some of the poorest countries in Europe, but I have never seen such wretchedness.'

Lizzie wondered at his words. 'You are well-travelled?'
'I am.'

'Where have you been?'

'I have journeyed through Portugal, Spain, Greece and Turkey. But this country, these people are more oppressed than any of those I have encountered abroad.' He paused and looked into her eyes. 'I can see that you are suffering. He placed a coin in her hand and closed her fingers around it.

'I can't accept—' Lizzie began.

'Think of it as a gift, from a stranger.'

Lizzie's eyes met his once more. Then she looked down at the coin in her palm. It would more than pay for another week's food. 'Thank you,' she whispered.

'You were on your way home, I think?' he said.

Lizzie nodded.

'I will see you safely to your door.'

He walked with her along the icy street until they reached her house. As they did so, Lizzie noticed that the man limped slightly. She unlocked the door. The man looked up at the sky. A solitary star was sparkling above the rooftops. She followed his gaze.

'It's beautiful, isn't it?' His breath formed delicate clouds.

Lizzie looked at him.

'If you need the aid of Captain Ludd, you may ask to speak to one of my fellows, a Mr Connor. He frequents the Angel Tavern. The landlady knows him, but not that he is a Luddite. You must be careful; there are informants everywhere. But take courage. All is not lost.'

He took her hand and kissed it through his scarf. Then he was gone.

NOVEMBER 1811

*O*nce the men had assembled in the Great Hall of Newstead Abbey, Lord Byron addressed them:

'Up until now you have been brave and that is commendable. However there is a fine line between bravery and foolhardiness. Many of you have been arrested and some have even died. In order for us to be effective, we must be organised. So, tonight I propose to turn us into a fighting force to be reckoned with. Now I know that some of you have never so much as traded blows in a brawl. I do not pretend that it will be without peril.'

Some of the men looked uneasy.

'We do have arms. Not many, but if we are disciplined and focused, I hope, we will not have to use them, except in the most desperate of circumstances.'

Byron walked into the centre of the group.

'I'm going to divide you up into regiments.'

'Like in the army?' a young lad asked.

Byron turned to him: 'Exactly like the army,' Byron said, 'because that is what we will be.' He moved to the other end of the hall.

'Form a circle,' he commanded. 'Facing inwards.' The men shuffled into a rough round.

'I'm going to put you into groups, and, if you all agree, give you numbers. You'll use these numbers instead of names. In the heat of battle it's easier to remember a number rather than a name. Plus, if any of us get apprehended, it will be difficult for the authorities to trace us. Does that sound reasonable?' The men nodded and made noises of co-operation.

Byron counted round the circle. 'There are twenty six of us. That makes three groups of eight, plus myself and this gentleman.' He indicated Peter Connor, who was standing to his left.

'Starting with me, one-one, one-two, one-three and so on up to one-zero. Then two-one, two-two, two-three,' he continued until he reached three-eight.

Byron could see that the men were remembering their numbers as he pointed to them. He decided to test them. 'You may find it simpler to think of your numbers as thirteen, fourteen and so on. You!' He pointed to one man: 'What is your number?'

'Twenty-six, sir.'

'Good. And you?'

'Thirty-three, sir.' This man even saluted.

'Marvellous!' Byron turned to Connor. 'Number Twelve, I think it's time to practise some military action.' Connor instructed Group One to move to one end of the hall and Group Three to the other. Group Two remained in the middle.

'The object,' Byron announced, 'is for the groups at either end to swap. The group in the centre, Group Two, your objective is to stop them. By any means possible. Go!'

Byron watched as the men tussled, shoved and tripped. After a while he could tolerate the shambles no longer. Neither group was making progress; nor were the members working together. 'Halt!' he called.

The men gradually became still, except for a pair of

them who were on the brink of a full-blown fight. Byron waded in and separated them. 'Gentlemen, please! This is just the sort of in-fighting that is going to scupper us.' He pushed them apart. As he did so, one of them gave Byron a hearty shove. Byron regained his balance and put up his fists: 'If you want a proper boxing match, I'd be glad to oblige.' Some of the men jeered and others gave cries of encouragement. 'Number twenty-three, isn't it?'

'That's right.' The man raised his fists. Byron circled him. Twenty-three, who was almost four inches taller than Byron, threw a punch. Byron ducked and caught him in the ribs. On his second attempt, Byron easily blocked him. He tried again and this time, as Byron blocked with his right arm, his other fist connected with twenty-three's chin. He lost his balance and toppled over. There was an enormous roar of approval. Twenty-three rubbed his jaw. Byron stepped over to him and held out his hand. With a look of bemused respect, twenty-three took it, and Byron helped him to his feet. He patted him on the back.

'There, sir. We must learn trust each other if we are to act together as one.'

'That were a damn good left hook!' twenty-three remarked, shaking Byron's hand. 'I'm glad you're on our side!' He turned to the others: 'Eh, lads?!' They laughed.

The younger lad spoke again: 'If we're your army, then you should be our captain.'

'Yes!' agreed twenty-three. 'Captain Ned Ludd!'

'Three cheers for Ned Ludd!'

All the men cheered. 'And down with all tyrants!'

Byron addressed them once again: 'Gentlemen, we are going to learn how to attack and defend. One group will attack and the others will defend. It will be like Thermopylae.'

'The moppy what?' asked twenty-three.

'The Gates of Fire,' Byron translated.

'I like the sound of that better.'

'Good! Group Two and Group Three will create a

funnel, through which Group One may enter and exit safely. You will close ranks once they are inside, and after we have eliminated the frames, give us safe passage outside again.'

'That don't sound too difficult,' twenty-three said, grinning.

'The difficult part will be if the Militia arrive before we're done,' twelve remarked.

'Of course,' Byron agreed. 'If that happens we shall have to make a hasty retreat; but not surrender. We will have a signal, so that we can escape as quickly as possible. Does anyone have any questions?'

The young lad raised his hand. 'There's not many of us, sir. There're loads of soldiers.'

Some of the men murmured agreement.

'If three hundred Spartans can take on the Persian army,' Byron smiled, 'I've every confidence we can succeed.'

Jack watched his father buckle the bridle over the grey horse's head. It chewed at the bit. Peter Connor shook his head. 'I won't let you get involved in framebreaking. I know what to do when engaged in battle; you don't.' He lifted the saddle onto the horse's back. 'I don't want to risk losing you.'

'Susan will think me a coward.'

Connor patted his son on the shoulder. 'Susan doesn't want a hero. She would much rather you were in one piece.'

Jack blushed. His father mounted the horse.

'Besides, if we do not return, we shall need you to bring the coach to town and collect our bodies.'

Jack frowned. Peter Connor nodded in the direction of the Abbey: 'Mr Fletcher will tell you where and when, should the need arise.'

The furrow in Jack's brow deepened.

'Don't worry, lad,' his father reassured him, 'I shan't

take any foolish risks.' He turned his horse toward Newstead. 'His Lordship's the one that needs protecting.'

'Have you read this?' Ben looked across the table toward his mother; she was holding up the newspaper.

'Don't tell me, Napoleon's invaded and we've all got to speak French.' He resumed eating.

'The latest incident of framebreaking: The soldiers were outnumbered by those calling themselves Luddites at Crosier's workshop in Bulwell. Apparently the Luddites referred to each other by numbers instead of names. They surrounded the soldiers and took their rifles from them. After breaking the frames they dragged the broken pieces into the yard where they burnt them, then they then returned the rifles to the soldiers, without ammunition.' She laid down her spectacles; taking up her wineglass she gulped the claret. She glanced at her son. Ben shrugged.

'What do they expect? This isn't just a gang of stupid peasants. Sounds to me like they know what they're doing.' He munched on a slice of pie: 'I believe that they're capable of anything.'

His mother laid down her knife and fork. 'Capable of killing?' she whispered.

Ben finished his meal and stood. 'Don't be afraid, Mother. Now that I'm the man of the house, I'll protect you.' He made to leave.

'Where are you going?' Mrs Harwood held onto her son's hand.

'To the Angel; then I have some business to attend to.' He kissed his mother on the cheek. 'It shouldn't take long.'

Through the twilight, Lizzie could hear the children's rhyme:

'Winding the bobbin up, winding the bobbin up, pull, pull, clap-clap-clap,
Now my work is nearly done, come with me and have some fun,

Winding the bobbin up, winding the bobbin up, pull, pull, clap, clap, clap.'

They sang, performing the actions that they had seen so many times, and work that they themselves would have to do once they were tall enough to reach the table.

Lizzie paired the stockings she had been seaming. Dusk was approaching. She closed the door and what little light had been shining weakly into her house disappeared. She squinted in the dark. Her eyes ached. She gave life to a candle which cast shadows that loomed around the walls. She fetched her comb and began to draw it through her hair. Whilst she was engaged in this simple task, her eyes wandered once more to the wooden box. How long had it been since she'd opened it? Small and dark, it looked insignificant in the warm light from the grate and the little candle.

She paused, unsure if she still believed any of it any more. Lizzie held her comb in front of the fire, pulled the hairs from it and tossed them into the flames. They burnt brightly for a second, and then were gone, leaving a faint acrid scent. She sat at the table and opened the box. The cards were cool and smooth to the touch. Lizzie closed her eyes. She cut the cards, placed one section on top of the other then shuffled them. She began to lay them out on the table before her.

Temperance: A picture of a woman mixing the contents of two goblets. This meant joining forces with someone, and to be prepared for confrontation. She placed the next card below the first. *Le Pendu*: The Hanged Man. This had to be Robert. His life hangs in the balance, she thought. The man on the card is upside down, but hung by his foot, not by his neck.

The next card was the Ten of Swords. Lizzie shuddered a little. Not a good card. It meant betrayal. Robert was not responsible for Mr Betts' death. Of that she was convinced. Ben had stabbed Robert in the back, as sure as the swords on the card had done so.

The Knight of Pentacles indicated the solution to the problem: A young dark-haired man, one who was unsure of his role in life but would be reliable and able to hold his ground in adversity. Have I already met this man, she wondered? She thought back to the stranger who had told her about foreign countries and given her the coin.

She turned the penultimate card in the spread. *Jugement*: The angel blows the trumpet on the last day. It was time for action. Time to accept past mistakes and embrace salvation.

The door opened. Lizzie, startled, jumped up and her chair toppled. Ben stood in the doorway. He closed the door behind him and stepped toward her.

'Did I frighten you?' His eyes shone in the firelight.

Lizzie shook her head. She was afraid that if she spoke her voice would betray her. She drew a deep breath. 'I'd offer you some tea, but I'm afraid we,' she checked herself, '*I* don't have any.'

'I don't care for tea anyway,' he said. 'I didn't come here for that.'

He was now standing so close to her that she could smell the beer on his breath. He raised his hand and stroked her cheek, his fingers cold and hard. Then he grasped her round the waist.

'You should keep your door locked, now that your brother's in gaol. You're all alone,' Ben reminded her. 'But you don't need to be. You don't need to be living here on your own without even tea to drink.' He stared into her eyes. Lizzie looked away from him; she tried to think of a way to release herself, but she could not.

He continued, 'I've always liked you, Lizzie. So pretty, so slender...' He moved his hand up and down her back. 'Too skinny now, though; you want feeding up, girl. I'd not see you starve.' Lizzie shivered. Although Ben was handsome, she feared he could be cruel.

'You marry me and you'll want for nothing. Now that my uncle's dead, I'll inherit the lot.' He noticed she was shivering. 'I'll make you warm, too.' He pulled her close to him and covered her mouth with his. He tasted of ale and onions. He drew his hands from her back and started to pull at her dress.

Momentarily released from his grip, Lizzie pushed him away as hard as she could. 'Leave me be!' she cried. He stumbled backwards, surprised by her strength.

'What?' he spluttered. 'Are you rejecting my proposal? Who do you think you are, Lizzie Molyneux? You French bitch. You'll be out on the street, then you'll be the new molly, Molyneux, and you'll have to serve all the men in Nottingham for a few pence. You don't have a choice, girl.'

He lunged for her and pinned her back against the table. 'If you won't marry me, I'll have you anyway, then you'll be ruined and no one will want you.'

She struggled as he started to hitch up her dress. He swiftly unbuttoned his breeches. She ceased to fight. 'Oh, you'll be good and lie still now, will you? Though I think I prefer it when you resist.' Ben grinned. Lizzie realised her chance. She reached down below her waist and took hold of him. He shut his eyes and groaned with pleasure. It immediately turned into a shriek of pain as she viciously tugged and squeezed. He stumbled over and she stood up. She seized a card from the table and showed it to him. 'There, Ben Harwood!' Her voice was a feral hiss. 'I'll not be your wife or your whore!' She held the card in front of his face until it was all he could see.

'The Ten of Swords: A man stabbed in the back. That's what you did to Robert. I'll die before you do it to me. Now get out!' She moved behind him and thrust him toward the door.

'You bitch!' Ben cried, 'You witch!' Lizzie could hear the fear in his voice.

'I'm not afraid of you,' she said, 'but you would do well

to be afraid of me!'

With that she pushed him out of the house and into the dark street. She slammed the door behind her and locked it. She stood alone inside, breathing hard. She returned to the table, turned over what would have been the final card. *La Force*: A young woman closing the jaws of a lion. She fought back a sob. She couldn't do this alone. She would have to ask someone for help.

> *The Angel*
> *Nottingham, 30 November 1811*

Dear Captain Ludd,

I pray that you will come to the aid of a young woman who at this present time is in a state of great distress. My brother is, as I write, in gaol. He was one of a group of frame breakers who most unluckily raided the workshop of Mr Betts. I say unluckily as they were attacked and apprehended by the militia when they tried to flee.

During the frame breaking one of the Luddites fired a shot at Mr Betts, the factory owner. He was killed. My brother was identified as the killer. I know he is innocent, as he has never fired a pistol in his life and would not know how to do so. Neither is he a murderer.

I plead for help, as I know you to be a man of honour and would wish to see justice done. One of your fellow Luddites met me only a few nights ago and gave me enough money to buy food. I am starving, as are all of us who have been made almost useless by the new frames. For every one in work, six have none. I ask not only for help for myself and for my brother, but for all the people who suffer unjustly.

Please write to me as soon as you are able. If you leave a letter for me at The Angel tavern, Stoney Street, Nottingham, then I shall fetch it from there. I shall go there every night just before the curfew at ten o'clock in order that I might collect it discreetly. I know one of your party drinks in the Angel, and I shall leave my letter with him to ensure it reaches you.

As you can see, I have mentioned few names but my own, in order to keep all of our arrangements secret. I entreat you, Captain Ludd, as one who loves Liberty, please, help us.

God protect the Trade.

Your humble servant,
Miss Lizette Molyneux (Stockinger)

DECEMBER 1811

At the corner of Stoney Street Lizzie waited until all the men had left The Angel for the night. She peered into the darkness. The fog was swirling round the windows, caught in the faint gleam from the lamps within. She did not want to be outside much longer. The curfew was fast approaching; a dire penalty awaited anyone out after that. The last man grunted a goodbye to the landlady and shuffled off down Woolpack Lane.

Lizzie felt her rosary against her chest. She touched the crucifix and hurried toward the tavern door, just as Emma was closing it.

'Lizzie!? What are you doing here? You should get home, it's so cold, and you'll be late.'

'There's something I must ask you.' The freezing air rasped in Lizzie's voice.

'Come inside, get in the warm.' Emma closed the door and led Lizzie into the smoky bar. She took a bottle of brandy from the shelf and poured a measure into a small tankard.

'Drink that; it'll warm you up.' Lizzie took a sip of the

sweet spirit. It burned her throat. 'Now, what's all this about?' Emma sat next to her.

'Is there a message for me? I wrote a letter...to Captain Ludd,' she whispered, 'I said to leave a note as to his reply, to be delivered here for me.'

'Good Lord, girl! What are you doing writing letters to a man that don't exist?'

'He does exist,' Lizzie insisted. 'I've spoken to him.'

Emma's eyes widened. 'Really? I thought he was like Robin Hood, just a character that people told stories about.'

'I swear he's a real man.' Lizzie took her rosary from beneath her shawl. 'I swear.'

Emma looked askance. There was a knock at the door. 'Who can that be at this hour? What do you want?' she called.

Lizzie concealed herself to one side of a dresser. A man's voice answered; it was quiet, but she still heard it.

'I have a message from Ned Ludd.'

Emma unlatched the door. 'Come in, quickly.' She ushered him inside. He was swathed in a black cloak, and a black silk scarf covered his face up to his eyes. Lizzie noticed that he limped slightly as he entered the room.

'There's someone here who has been writing to him,' Emma said.

'They seem to have vanished.' His voice was gentle and well-spoken. Lizzie recognised it. She stepped out.

'I'm Lizette Molyneux. I need to talk to you.' The man's eyes showed that he was smiling.

'We can't talk here, Lizette. We must go somewhere safer.' He gestured to Lizzie. 'Please, come with me, and we'll discuss this elsewhere.' He turned to Emma: 'Thank you for your hospitality.' He bowed slightly. Then he put his arm around Lizzie's shoulders. 'I'll look after her,' he said to Emma. Emma put her hand over her mouth. 'Captain Ludd!'

'Tell no one,' he whispered as he led Lizzie into the

street. Emma shook her head. Then the two of them were concealed by the fog.

At the bottom of the street, Lizzie could just make out the outline of a coach waiting for them. She noticed a crest on the door. The man opened it and Lizzie climbed in. She heard him say something like 'Home' to the driver, but nothing else to indicate where they were going. Once inside the coach, the stranger removed the scarf from his face. He was young, a few years older than Lizzie, pale skinned, with dark blue eyes and long eyelashes. He removed one of his gloves and she could see a beautiful ring and his smooth hand with bitten fingernails. He took her hand. 'I received your letter. I believe your brother is in grave danger.'

Lizzie nodded. 'He was arrested for frame breaking and faces transportation, and now there're rumours of execution.'

The coach left Nottingham, turning up the Mansfield Road. Lizzie could tell that they were climbing the hill and heading out of town.

'I didn't know what else to do. I warned him not to get caught, but he was unlucky.'

'He's lucky to have you for a sister.' Despite the darkness, Lizzie could see that he was very handsome and she realised that he still held her hand. She looked out the window. 'Where are we going?' she asked.

'Newstead,' the man replied.

'Why there?'

'It's where I live.'

Lizzie had never been this far out of Nottingham, and yet it seemed a normal journey for the stranger. Hadn't he said he had been abroad?

The man's voice was gentle: 'When did you last eat? You must be starving.' Lizzie nodded. The fog had lifted and the moon was now shining into the carriage. He wasn't just handsome, he was beautiful. She felt her cheeks redden.

When they reached Ravenshead the coach turned left off the main road and descended down a long lane lined with trees. In the distance Lizzie saw a lake, the moon reflected in the peaceful water. Facing the lake was a large stone building with what looked like a great ruined church window on the left and stone steps leading to the main door in the right hand corner of the courtyard. The house seemed enormous. The man swept out of the coach and helped Lizzie down the step. He closed the carriage door and called out to thank the driver. As he led Lizzie across the courtyard his limp seemed more pronounced.

'It's freezing. Let me get you something to eat and drink, and we'll talk more once inside.'

He showed her into the Great Hall. A raven, perched on the empty fireplace, flapped its wings and squawked a greeting. The man led her to a smaller dining room, where a table had been laid for two people. On the table there was cutlery and a tureen that was resting in a heavy iron basin, which looked to be filled with hot water. A fire was burning in the large grate. Lizzie noticed a huge dog lying by the fire. As they entered, it stretched, stood and padded over. Lizzie froze, terrified. The man crouched down to the dog, took its head in his hands and spoke softly to it. 'Now, Wolf, I hope you're going to behave; we have a guest this evening.' The dog panted and wagged its tail. The man patted him affectionately, and then turned to Lizzie. Noticing that she was uneasy, he said, 'There's nothing to fear. He's as soft as a sheep. Honestly!' She was shivering as he took off his cloak. 'Please,' he said, 'sit by the fire.' She put her bag down and sat. The dog pottered over to her and rested its head on the arm of the chair. 'There... You see?'

Lizzie looked at the dog. It was long legged, with a reddish brown rough coat. Its eyebrows seemed to be constantly moving, but it didn't look fierce, only inquisitive.

The man took a slender poker from the fire and slowly

slid it into an open bottle of wine. He poured two glasses. He sat in the carved mahogany chair opposite Lizzie. 'Here,' he said, passing her one of the glasses, 'it's Portuguese wine. I brought it from Lisbon.' Lizzie took a small mouthful. It was warm and comforting.

'It's delicious,' she said. She looked around the room. The walls were panelled and the ceiling carved like a chapel. 'Is this your home? It doesn't look like somewhere a frame breaker would live. Who are you?'

The dog turned its attention to its master. The man stroked the dog's head and smiled.

'I am George Gordon, the sixth Lord Byron. This is my ancestral home, Newstead Abbey. My family has lived here for almost three hundred years, and by a stroke of fortune I inherited it when I was ten years old.'

Lizzie almost dropped her glass. 'Lord Byron?' she whispered.

Byron smiled. 'And who are you, Lizette Molyneux? That is not a common name.'

'Please, call me Lizzie, my Lord.'

'I will call you Lizzie, if you promise to call me George, or Byron. You don't need to bother with titles. But please, tell me about yourself.'

'My brother Robert and I are twins. Our mother died giving birth to us. Our father fled France after the Revolution.'

'That explains your name. A child of the Revolution. *Magnifique*!'

Lizzie drew her rosary from her bodice. 'This belonged to my mother.' She held up the claret coloured beads. The gold crucifix glittered in the firelight. 'My father gave it to her as a wedding gift. It was one of the few things he managed to bring with him when he escaped.'

Byron leaned over to look at it. 'It's beautiful,' he said. He took the rosary from her and placed it round his own neck. Lizzie was aware of her heart racing; she could feel the effect of the wine in her blood. Somewhere a clock chimed midnight. He took her hand. 'Come and have some food.' He led her to the table.

He passed her a bowl filled with little fruits. They looked like black cherries, but smelt savoury.

'What are they?' Lizzie asked.

'Olives,' Byron replied. He placed one in his mouth and removed the stone. 'Be careful, they have a pit in the middle.' She took one and followed his lead.

'They're lovely,' she said.

Byron tore off a large piece of crusty bread, spread some butter on it and handed it to her. Lizzie didn't want to seem impolite, but she couldn't help gobbling the bread down. Byron removed the lid from the tureen and ladled some of the broth into a bowl for her. 'My servants have prepared some carrot and barley soup. I trust it is to your liking.'

Lizzie took one of the silver spoons and began to eat. After a while she noticed that Byron had eaten very little by comparison. She blushed. 'I'm sorry, I must seem greedy.'

'Not at all,' he said. 'I'm glad to share what I have with you. I hate to see someone go hungry. Have you eaten enough now?' Lizzie nodded.

'Let's have some more wine.' Byron poured out another glassful. 'They told me abroad that it doesn't travel well, but I think it tastes just as wonderful as it did there.'

'My rosary isn't the only thing my father brought from France,' she said.

Byron raised an eyebrow as Lizzie fetched her bag and drew out the small wooden box. 'They're cards,' she said, opening the lid.

'How interesting... Playing cards?'

'No, they're Tarot cards. They were made for the Marquis De Condorcet. He gave them to my father as payment for his last work.'

Byron took one of the cards: *La Lune*. 'What work did your father do?'

'He was a tailor, to the aristocracy, so of course after the Revolution he was in great danger. The Marquis had nothing left to give him as payment, so he gave him the cards.'

'What do you use them for?'

'I read fortunes.'

Byron's eyes sparkled in the firelight. 'Would you read my fortune?'

'Are you sure? The cards don't always tell us what we want to know.'

'I am not afraid,' said Byron, 'I'm fascinated.'

'Very well then,' said Lizzie, 'I'll do it.'

He stood, picked up the wine glasses and moved towards the door at the other side of the room. 'Follow me,' he said. 'And bring the candles, it's damnably dark on the stairs.'

Lizzie took the silver candlestick from the table. The three flames fluttered as Byron led her through the silent corridor and up the narrow spiral of stone steps. Lizzie noticed the little stained glass windows in the stairwell, Medieval images that made her think of a shrine. Byron seemed to find it awkward ascending the stairs; every other step he leaned slightly against the wall for support. They crossed an almost empty anteroom .

'My inner sanctum,' Byron announced, as he pushed opened the bedroom door. Lizzie stood motionless for a moment. The large bed had four wooden posts, hung with heavy tapestry curtains, which like its cover, displayed beautiful workmanship. She felt soft carpet beneath her feet. Byron placed the glasses on a table near the window, the curtains had been drawn but a shaft of moonlight was gleaming through a gap in the centre. A generous fire burning in the corner sent sparks up the chimney. Lizzie was unsure if it was her imagination, but she thought she smelled church incense.

Byron closed the door behind her, took the candlestick and placed it on the table. She was still holding the small card box. Byron drew up a chair, sat and pulled off his boots with some difficulty. He patted the seat next to him.

'*Ela*,' he said, smiling. 'It's Greek. 'It means, *come here*.'

Lizzie sat down and opened the box. She gave the pack to Byron. 'You need to shuffle them, and cut them. Then I'll deal the spread.'

Byron took a sip of wine before he expertly shuffled the cards. 'I feel like I'm at the club in London,' he said. 'Are you going to deal me a winning hand?' Catching sight of Lizzie's serious expression he checked himself: 'I'm sorry, I confess I am a little nervous.' He cut the cards.

Lizzie dealt them face down. 'The card at the centre is the inquirer,' she said. 'That's you. The card at the bottom is the past.' She placed this card below the first card. 'The card on the left is the present problem, and on the right is its solution.' She dealt two more. 'The next card is the immediate future and the final card is the far future.' She placed these above the first card. The formation of a St. Peter's cross.

Lizzie turned the first card: 'The King of Cups.'

'Is that me?' Byron asked. Lizzie nodded. The card depicted a young-looking king holding a large jeweled goblet.

'You enjoy sensation, you are a loving man, but you wear your heart on your sleeve. You need to be careful with whom you fall in love.'

Byron drew a breath. 'Good Lord!' He leaned his chin on his hand. Lizzie turned the second card, the Four of Swords. The four vertical weapons on the card looked as though they had their points thrust into the ground at the corners of a rectangle. 'You've suffered loss in the past—the recent past.'

'My mother,' Byron said quietly. 'She died in the summer. And one of my best friends, Charles Matthews, drowned himself.'

'I'm sorry,' said Lizzie. 'Do you want me to stop?'

'No, please, go on.' He took a deep breath and steeled

himself.

'The third card is the present problem.' It was the moon again. *La Lune*. 'It can signify hidden danger, but it can also mean secret feelings, unspoken love.'

Byron gazed at the card. The full moon depicted was now watching them from the window. Byron looked up and his eyes met Lizzie's. She looked down at the table and turned the fourth card.

'This is the solution to the present problem. *Les Amouraux*. The Lovers.'

They both held their breath.

Byron stood up. 'Please, read the final cards,' he said. He seized his wine glass and drained it. 'Please, read them,' he implored her. She turned over the penultimate card.

'*Le Monde*. The World. It means success and recognition.'

'My poem, 'Childe Harold', shall be published next year. Does that mean that it will be well received?'

'More than that,' said Lizzie, 'it means adoration, worship. '

He quickly pulled his shirt over his head; her crucifix still hung round his neck. His broad chest was covered with downy dark hair. He smiled as he leaned over the table. 'Show me the far future!'

Lizzie hesitated. She had a feeling that it might not be what he expected.

'*Le Diable*. The Devil.'

Byron laughed, nervously. 'Is that what I become? Or does it mean I am already damned?' His expression reminded Lizzie of the raven in the hall. She shook her head: 'Not damnation,' she said, 'but it can mean an illness. Or it can mean a life cut short.'

'That settles it!' His voice was firm, determined. 'If I am to be denied a long life, I'd better enjoy this world as much as I can before I move on to the next, whether heaven or hell. He kissed her slowly and deliberately, with a passion she had never felt before. His mouth was warm, he tasted of wine. Something ignited inside her, like a lamp being lit. She ran her hands through his hair and grasped his back. He clasped her to him and she could feel his desire pressing against her.

He unlaced her dress and guided her to the bed. He gently laid her down. Lizzie was acutely aware of every sensation, and her entire body tingled with an aching need. Byron reached down and removed her shoes, and then he lifted her chemise. He slid his hand upwards, above the top of her stockings, between her thighs. The sensation was divine. She reached for him, drew his face to hers and kissed him. His mouth was hot, his movements slow and sensual. He undid the buttons on her chemise and his tongue traced her breasts. Breathing hard, Lizzie stroked his back, her fingers found small moles and tiny scars. He had survived some disease. She prayed that he would live longer than the cards predicted.

Byron unbuttoned his breeches. He stripped them off together with his stockings and dropped them on the floor. Then he turned to Lizzie.

'I will be as gentle as I can,' he said. 'I won't lie to you, it may hurt a little, but only for a moment.' He stroked her cheek, and then he parted her legs and lay over her. Lizzie felt as though she were on a cliff top, afraid to fall, but yearning to see over the edge, even to step over. She felt him enter her. And then she felt something give deep within her. She gasped. He kissed her and withdrew slightly.

'Do you want me to stop?' he asked.

'No,' she breathed. 'No, I want you.'

She felt a keen pang of lust as he slid into her completely. He sighed with pleasure. Their bodies began to move in rhythm. Lizzie closed her eyes. Now she knew why people shut their eyes when kissing: it was to fully enjoy the physical sensation.

Byron measured his movements until he was gliding,

exquisitely, slowly. She opened her eyes and saw that he was gazing at her.

'You are so alive, Lizzie,' he whispered. 'You make me feel alive.'

Her rosary hung from his neck, trailing over her breasts and swinging back and forth with movements of his body. Her hips rose to meet his. Lizzie knew that what they were doing was sinful. She addressed the crucifix; how could something so beautiful be wrong? She wondered if she had said it out loud, because Byron answered her:

'There is no sin. This is all there is. This is why we are alive.'

He turned onto his back and pulled her on top of him. Lizzie removed her chemise.

'We are half dust, half deity, and this is the closest we ever get to heaven,' Byron gasped. 'Do you feel it?'

'Yes!' Lizzie was almost breathless.

She clasped Byron's shoulders and their hips pressed together. He cried out: '*Thay-ah mou!* Lizzie, my goddess!' Tiny beads of sweat sparkled on his forehead. They were both panting. Lizzie put her lips to his once more. She kissed him with all her strength. He held her tightly until the powerful sensations subsided.

After a while of lying motionless, Lizzie looked down the bed at their feet. Hers were still covered by her stockings, his were naked. Lizzie remembered how he limped when walking. One of his feet seemed much smaller than the other. He realised that she was looking at it.

'I am cursed and deformed.'

'No, Byron,' she reassured him, 'you are beautiful.' The moonlight was glowing on his body. 'You are like a statue, a beautiful living statue.'

'It is your passion that has enlivened me,' he murmured. 'Thank you, Lizzie. You have given me something very rare and precious.' He kissed her again. Then he drew the heavy bedclothes around them and they slept.

Lizzie woke to hear the sound of water being poured. She opened her eyes and reached out across the bed, but she was alone. Her fingers touched the beads of her rosary which was now lying on the pillow next to her. The door opened, but instead of Byron, a young woman entered. She placed some towels on the chair and opened the curtains.

'Morning, Miss,' she smiled. Her accent was Welsh. 'What a lovely day, bright sun, frosty grass. I love it when it's like this.'

Lizzie guessed the girl was a little older and taller than herself. She turned to face Lizzie and giggled. 'I see Queen Mab hath been with you!'

Lizzie didn't know what to do. She gathered the sheets around her, dumbfounded.

"I'm Susan.' The girl sat on the bed. She put out her hand. 'What's your name?'

'Lizzie.'

Susan shook her hand gently. 'Well, Lizzie, aren't you the lucky one?' The girl was still smiling. She didn't appear at all shocked or even surprised. 'His Lordship asked me to get you a bath. Best leave it a while; it's red hot at the moment.' Susan stood up and picked up the pile of towels from the chair and hung them over a rail. She poked the fire vigorously, stirring up sparks. Then she moved the rail closer to it.

'He don't do it with everyone, you know,' Susan said.

'What do you mean?' Lizzie asked, knowing perfectly well what Susan was referring to.

'Lord Byron!' She looked out of the window. 'What I mean is, he likes both boys and girls, but not *every* boy, or *every* girl.'

'I see.' Lizzie was at a loss as to what else she could say.

Susan's face was sprinkled with light freckles. She was obviously well fed. Her arms looked strong. She took

Lizzie's hand once more.

'I reckon you are the prettiest girl I've ever seen. Even if you are a bit, well, slender.' Her voice was kind. 'He don't like us too thin or too fat. Nor too old or too young. How old *are* you?'

'Eighteen.'

'I'm only two years older than you.' Susan grinned. 'I'm nearly the same age as his Lordship. He's in such a good mood this morning. You certainly pleased him.'

Lizzie blinked.

Susan warmed to her subject. 'Isn't it the most wonderful thing? And isn't he marvellous at it?'

Lizzie could feel her cheeks aflame. Susan's eyes were shining.

'You did enjoy it, didn't you?'

Lizzie nodded. Susan leaned back on the bed. A look of realisation crept over her.

'Oh, my goodness. It was your first time, wasn't it? Your first ever? And here I am chatting on as if you're just like me.'

Lizzie found her voice. 'Have you made love with other men?'

'You talk very genteel,' Susan remarked. 'He'd love that. Yes, to answer you, I have. A couple of lads from Linby. Just a tumble really. I'll probably end up marrying one of them. Different with *him*, though.' Susan nodded towards the desk. Byron's boots were under the chair. Lizzie suddenly felt a sharp pang of emotion and excitement. She could feel him. She remembered his sensitive mouth on her neck, the look on his face when he...

'When he does it, it's special.' Susan smiled. 'You should call yourself *Lucky Lizzie*.' She stood. 'I reckon your bath will be just right now; not too hot, not too cold.'

Susan moved to the desk to pick up the empty wineglasses. She noticed Lizzie's cards. 'They're strange,' she said. 'I've seen his Lordship play cards before, but not like those.' She picked one up: '*La Lune?*' she read. Then another: 'Les Am-our-aux.' She raised her eyebrows at the picture of the naked lovers and glanced at Lizzie.

'They're mine.' Lizzie was nervous about someone else touching them.

Susan hummed a little tune. 'Well, aren't you full of secrets!' Lizzie bit her lip. Susan examined *The Lovers* card. 'What are they for? Are they magic?'

'In a way, I suppose you could call them that.' Lizzie stood up.

'Here, you'll catch your death.' Susan slipped Byron's embroidered silk dressing robe around Lizzie's naked shoulders and tied the cord at her waist.

'They mean different things. They're not all they seem at first glance.'

Susan caught Lizzie's eye. 'Like most things,' she said, 'or at least, most people.' She drew her breath sharply. 'Are you a fortune teller? Did you tell Byron's fortune?'

The door to the stairs opened. 'Speak of the devil!' Susan whispered.

'Susan, have you prepared Miss Molyneux's bath?' Byron asked.

Susan smiled and bobbed a little curtsey. 'Of course m'lord.'

'Thank you.'

Lizzie saw that Byron was wearing a fine shirt, dark moleskin breeches and little slippers. She watched as he stepped toward Susan and kissed her forehead.

'I think I'll have eggs for breakfast, Susan. Be sure you make enough for both of us. I'm ravenous this morning!' He glanced toward Lizzie. Lizzie blushed. Byron continued, 'Leave it say, half an hour or so, in order for Miss Molyneux to enjoy her bath?'

Susan grinned. 'As you wish, sir.' Then she was gone.

Byron turned to Lizzie. 'My robe suits you.' He looked down at the cards on the table and then back at her. 'Come here,' he murmured. Lizzie's feet felt the soft Turkish carpet. Byron put his arms around her and stroked her hair.

'*Zou-e mou sas agapo*,' he said. Lizzie looked up at him. 'It means, my life I love you.'

She rested her head on his shoulder.

'You better have your bath,' he said, 'before it goes cold.' Byron nodded toward the towel rail. 'Susan always warms the towels for me. She is good.' He lifted Lizzie's chin and then untied the robe. 'Not as good, nor as bad, as you though.' He smiled and slipped his hands round Lizzie's waist then kissed her tenderly.

'I meant everything I said last night. I will do my level best to help you, Lizzie.' He looked into her eyes.

'Thank you,' Lizzie said.

'Well thank you for enlightening me. Now, don't take *too* long getting dressed. Susan will have our breakfast ready by half past eleven.'

Byron took his jacket from the chair and disappeared down the stairs.

Robert's throat was parched and sore as though he'd swallowed broken glass. He was cold to his bones. He had slept little on the hard bench, yet his dreams had been of a warm fire and a soft bed. He shivered and yawned at the same time. The heavy door of his cell grated open and two men entered. The younger had the face of a terrier, white with reddish hair. 'I won't bid you good morning, because it's not. Least not for you.'

In silence the other man fixed Robert's gaze with a gargoyle's glare.

'Do you know the penalty for wreckin'?' The terrier asked.

Robert shook his head.

'Liar. You must have seen this.'

He unrolled a copy of the poster that Robert had held up in the graveyard.

'Transportation! That means going away, a long ways away. And we've got word from London that the punishment's going to be made harsher,' he sneered. 'Either way, lad, you'll be facing the gallows.'

Robert's thoughts immediately ran to Lizzie; she'd be alone.

'You've got a sister, haven't you?'

'Yes.' Robert's voice was a rasp.

'What d'you think'll happen to her without your protection? Never mind the shame of a convict on her.' Robert leapt to his feet. He was about to throw a punch when the gargoyle seized him and forced him to sit again.

'You're hot-blooded, Molyneux. But then you foreigners are,' the terrier snarled. 'You're all the same. But I will not see French-style mobs in my country, let alone in my city. You're already accused of murder; you're only making things worse for yourself.' He pulled up the small wooden stool which was the only other stick of furniture. 'So now, you're going to tell me who your fellows are...'

Robert remembered a word often used by his father: '*Jamais.*'

'Sammy? Jamie?' the terrier asked. 'Jamie who?'

Robert gave a snort of derision.

'Don't mock me, you'll regret it.'

The gargoyle twisted Robert's arm behind his back and gripped his chin, pushing it over the opposite shoulder. He could feel his tendons stretching. 'Tell me their names!'

Robert croaked for breath. 'Never!'

The terrier waved his hand and the brute released him.

'*Jamais*! Never!'

Leaning close to Robert the terrier's bitter, pale eyes pierced him. 'I'm glad. Because you'll be hanged. And it would make me sick at heart for a bead-jiggling Frenchman to go free.'

Lizzie sipped the hot, aromatic tea from a fine china cup, the steam rising from it obscuring her view slightly. Byron, seated at the end of the table, in the chair he had occupied the night before, ate with enthusiasm. Wolf sat close by him, his eyes fixed on his master, giving a plaintiff whine. Byron took his last piece of bread, dipped it in the yolk of an egg and fed it to him. The dog snaffled it, licking Byron's fingers. Lizzie smiled. She finished her omelet and sat back in her chair. Byron pushed his empty plate away.

'Now,' he said, wiping his fingers on a napkin, 'I've been thinking about your problem. Your brother is in gaol at the moment, isn't he?'

'He is,' she frowned. What sort of breakfast would he be having?

'So, you're alone...' His expression was serious, his eyes the slate grey blue of the lake. 'But you're not alone, Lizzie. I am resolved to assist you.'

Lizzie opened her mouth to speak, but found she could not. There was a sudden, searing pain along her arm and up into her neck. She gasped for breath. The dog began to whine again. Byron moved to her in an instant.

'What is it?'

As quickly as the pain had arrived it was gone. Lizzie felt released; she relaxed a little in the chair and looked at him.

'It's Robert. I know he is suffering.'

Byron took her hand. 'You can feel his pain?'

'It has happened before,' she admitted, 'when we were children. I was making tea and I suddenly felt a terrible pain in my head, and then in my back. I dropped the milk jug. Our father was about to scold me for being clumsy, but he realised something was wrong. At that moment, one of Robert's friends ran into the house, crying. Robert had fallen out of a tree. He'd hit his head, and landed on his back.'

Byron curled his arm around Lizzie's shoulders. He wondered what would happen if Robert were to be executed.

'Listen to me!' he said as he held her tightly. 'We are going to get your brother out of there, I swear to you.' He felt tears spring to his eyes. He blinked them away, and kissed Lizzie's cheek. 'I'm going to protect you, but first I'm going to teach you how to protect yourself.'

Lizzie watched as he took a large wooden box from the sideboard. He opened it and inside, nestling in soft brown velvet, were two ornate pistols. Byron removed them both from the box and held them up for her to see.

'You are right handed, I think?'

Lizzie nodded. Byron returned the pistols to the box and picked it up.

'Come with me,' he said.

They moved into the Long Gallery, the wintry sunshine throwing pale pools of light onto the creaking wooden floor. Outside Lizzie noticed a second smaller lake, more like a large ornamental pond with trees beyond.

Byron poured powder into the barrel, dropped the ball into it and jabbed it in securely with a thin metal rod. 'That's Devil's Wood,' he remarked as he loaded his pistol, 'where a monk once bumped into Beelzebub.' He added powder to the flash pan, cocked the pistol and walked to the middle of the room. 'Now watch.'

He stretched out his arm. 'Always turn sideways; it gives your opponent a smaller target.' He firmly squeezed the trigger. There was a loud crack and instantly a brandy glass on the shelf at the other end of the room splintered, the shards of glass glittering as they sprayed onto the floor.

Lizzie's ears were ringing. The sulphuric scent of gunpowder was pungent in the cold air. Wolf began to bark. Byron shouted. 'Fletcher!' His man servant hurried into the hall.

'Take Wolf out for a walk, would you? He's becoming agitated.'

The fine lines around Fletcher's eyes crinkled as he smiled at Lizzie. 'Very good m'lord.'.

'I am teaching Miss Molyneux how to fight a duel,' he announced, as though he were explaining the rules of cricket.

'Course you are m'lord.' Fletcher gave a little bow to Lizzie and disappeared through the corridor to the dining room. Lizzie could hear him talking to the dog. 'You been frightened by his Lordship? You and me both, lad.'

Byron reloaded the pistol. He approached Lizzie: 'It's your turn.' He placed the pistol into her right hand. It was warm and ominously heavy. It felt totally alien, a deadly piece of machinery. He stood behind her and positioned her arm.

'Concentrate,' he murmured. He kissed her neck. 'Breathe deeply and slowly. If you're tense, you'll shake. Hold your breath when you fire. Aim for that bottle.'

He slipped his hand over hers and guided it to the left slightly. Lizzie felt her heart pushing through her chest. Byron curled his fingers around hers and helped her pull the trigger. Immediately the bottle exploded, scattering jewels of green glass.

'Good shot!' Byron exclaimed. He took the pistol and reloaded it. 'On your own this time!' He handed it back to her. He looked around for something to use as a target. 'Just a moment...' He snatched up a little book that was lying on a seat near one of the windows. 'Perfect!' He grinned. Lizzie noticed the name of the author on the cover: R. Southey.

'You can show Mr. Southey exactly what we think of him.' Byron hobbled to the other end of the gallery and stood the book on the shelf, the front cover facing outwards. He retreated behind Lizzie. 'Whenever you're ready; fire!'

The gun felt even heavier now that she was holding it on her own. Lizzie focused all her energy on the target. She drew her fingers in tightly and felt the mechanism snap like a thunderclap. The ball pierced the book. Byron was ecstatic.

'*Thav-massia!*' he cried. 'You've a natural talent, unlike Mr. Southey.' He hurried over and fetched the book. There was a hole right through it. He gave it to her in exchange for the pistol.

'Keep that as a souvenir; and I have something else for you.' He opened a drawer at the bottom of the pistol case. Lizzie hadn't noticed it until now. He drew out a small silver gun, etched with delicate filigree.

'This is a lady's pistol. I have no idea for whom it was made originally, but today, it's yours.'

He placed it in her hand. Lizzie admired it. 'It's beautiful,' she said.

'I'll show you how to load it,' Byron said.

The carriage drew to a halt at the bottom of Barker Gate. Peter Connor climbed down from the driver's seat and stood ready to open the door for Lizzie. Byron took her hand.

'Make sure you look after yourself. Keep your pistol loaded, and above all, dry.'

Her eyes met his. He smiled. 'Do not fear, I will return to help you as soon as I can.' He planted a sensuous kiss in her palm.

'Where are you going now?' she asked.

'To the hospital,' he sighed. 'I am to have my lame foot trussed up again. A regular necessity ever since childhood. And a damn nuisance.'

Lizzie thought of the moonlight glowing on his body: 'Remember what I said,' she whispered, 'you are beautiful, Byron.'

'And you, I think, are one of the kindest girls that I have ever... And I will not say goodbye, so let this be *au revoir*.'

Lizzie nodded, '*Au revoir*,' she said.

A gust of cold air embraced her as she descended the carriage step. Connor touched the brim of his hat to her. Then he closed the door and took his seat once more. Lizzie watched as they drove away. She stood for a few minutes, observing the townspeople going about their business. Women with their baskets full of groceries, a baker with a tray of pies, a pair of smart gentlemen discussing the price of property. How ordinary it all seemed, and how extraordinary the last twenty-four hours had been for her.

'Mama,' Caroline Elliott said as she looked up from peeling carrots, 'shall we invite Lizzie to spend Christmas Day with us?'

Joan smiled at her daughter, 'That's a lovely idea, Caro, but I'm not sure we'd have enough food.'

'Please, Mama!' Michael put down his toy horse that had been galloping across the rug: 'Please let's have Lizzie here. She can have my dinner.'

The girls laughed at their little brother.

'Somehow I don't think you'd give up your Christmas dinner.' Rose gave him a playful shove.

'That's very kind,' Joan said as she picked him up and sat him on her knee.

'Perhaps Lizzie could bring some food with her?' suggested Sophie. Dora grinned: 'Ask her to bring plum pudding.' Mary agreed. 'Plum pudding!' she cried.

'Alright,' Joan nodded, 'that's a good idea. Caro, you and Ellie go round to Lizzie and invite her.'

The girls jumped up, wrapped themselves in woollen shawls and hurried out.

Lizzie poked the fire. It had taken her much longer than usual to build and light it. Finally the golden flames flickered to life. She rubbed her hands over it, and gazing into the grate her mind wandered. She remembered the fire at Newstead, reading the cards to Byron, the warmth of his body against hers. She opened her eyes and noticed her father's portrait.

'It was not wrong, Papa. It didn't feel wrong. He did not hurt me or force me. He only did what we both wanted.'

She took the pistol from her bag, together with a small

vial of gunpowder, and a pouch containing the lead bullets. She placed them in a drawer of the dresser. She removed the box of cards and placed them in the drawer also. She felt something else in her bag. It was a small leather purse; she did not recognise it. Opening it she discovered several coins and a tiny folded piece of paper. She unfolded it and read Byron's handwriting:

This is not payment. Think of it as a gift, from a stranger. B

She kissed the note. 'Thank you,' she murmured.

Lizzie sat down at the frame. She threaded the needles and set to work. The thread rattled its way across from right to left. She pushed the frame forward and created neat rows of stitches. She had a day's work on which to catch up.

'There will never be any improvement, will there?' Byron shifted his weight from one foot to the other, stamping his feet firmly into his boots. His lame foot was encased once more, bound and trussed.

'I'm afraid not, my lord,' Doctor Markham said, 'but it is only a mild deformity; you are fortunate that you are able to walk tolerably well.'

'And ride, and swim, and everything else that a man should be able to do.' Byron gave the doctor a knowing smile: 'And all of those I do better than most.'

'There does tend to be, how shall I put this, a certain compensation. If there is weakness in one organ of the body, there is often an exceptional strength in other parts. Those born blind often have an unusual sensitivity to touch and so forth.'

Byron grinned. 'You have hit the nail squarely on the head. Perhaps you should be a carpenter as well as a doctor.'

The physician laughed. 'I do not think that my patients

would want me nailing them back together. Although, I do believe that broken or deformed bones would benefit from some sort of internal splint. If that were possible, your foot might have been corrected soon after you were born.'

Byron's eyes widened: 'Really? Good heavens, what a thought. Metal bones...' He pondered for a moment. 'Mind you, had I not been cursed in this way, I may not have been so keen to excel on the sports field, or in the bedroom.' He shot the doctor a sharp glance. The physician coughed politely: 'Your functions in that area are satisfactory, I take it?'

Byron smiled. 'I have never had any complaint. Although, a few years ago, my doctor in Southwell told me that perhaps four times in one day was rather excessive, and causing me to be exhausted.'

The doctor raised his eyebrows: 'My lord, I take it that you have eased off a little now?'

'A little,' Byron nodded. 'I try to restrict myself to twice in twenty-four hours, if I can,' he quipped. 'Being virtually alone at Newstead for the last few months I have been living the life of a monk. Well, almost...' As Byron walked towards the door, Doctor Markham stood and bowed.

'You know,' Byron sighed as he left the room, 'if you could prescribe a cure for being in love, you really would make your fortune.'

'Mama sent us to ask you to come to our house for Christmas Day!' Caroline and Ellie smiled as Lizzie brought them into the kitchen.

'Well, that's very kind. I accept your invitation.'

Lizzie made some tea for them.

'It's only a few days away. We sang carols in church last Sunday,' Ellie was beaming. She gulped her tea. 'You're so lucky to have milk in your tea.'

Lizzie frowned. 'Do you not have any? My goodness, I will send you home with a jug of milk.'

'Mama had to ask the vicar for some money, so we can

buy food.' Ellie looked at her sister, and Caroline nodded. 'Ever since Papa died...'

Lizzie wondered what she could do to help. She stood, opened the drawer of the dresser and took out two of the six silver coins that Byron had given her. 'Here you are!' She laid them on the table, one in front of each of the girls. The sisters looked at each other wide-eyed. 'Please, take them.' Lizzie poured another cup of tea. Caroline picked up the coin and examined it: 'A whole shilling each?'

Lizzie nodded: 'I did some extra work, and there's only me here at the moment, so I can spare it.'

'Thank you, Lizzie.'

'You're very welcome.' There was a moment's silence.

'Will you bring some food with you on Christmas Day?' Ellie asked.

'Of course, what would you like me to bring?'

The girls exchanged a look: 'Plum pudding!' they chorused and giggled.

Lizzie laughed. 'Certainly! I will make the best plum pudding you have ever eaten.'

'I expected a greeting from a Benedictine or Carthusian Friar!' Francis Hodgson embraced Byron on the icy abbey steps.

Byron laughed, 'You must know me well enough to understand that I could never adopt a celibate life. Welcome to my gothic ruin.'

A second, younger man gingerly ascended the slippery steps. 'Heavens, George, how on earth do you manage these treacherous stairs?'

Byron held out his hand to him: 'Take my arm, Will. To answer your question, I seldom venture out into the frozen wastes. I prefer to cling to my fireside with a good bottle of claret.'

'Alone?' William Harness shot his friend a quizzical glance.

'For the most part, yes; however, I do have company on occasion.'

'Someone to share your wine?'

Byron nodded as he showed them indoors, 'My cellar, my larder and my home is yours, for the duration.' They passed through the Great Hall and into the dining room. Byron indicated Wolf who was snoring by the fire, his legs twitching slightly as he dreamt.

'You see what an effective guard dog I have.'

Will laughed and patted the sleeping animal. Byron poured large glasses of brandy for them.

'I propose a toast,' Francis proclaimed as he raised his glass, 'to absent friends.'

They gulped the brandy.

'And a second toast!' Will Harness offered: 'To Harrow School, to Byron, and to Cambridge, our seats of learning and licentiousness!'

Byron clinked his glass against Will's: 'Amen to that!'

The three friends made themselves comfortable in chairs around the hearth.

'Another Christmas, George, another year gone,' Francis observed. Byron sighed, 'I will be twenty-four in a few weeks' time—almost a quarter of a century.'

'Are you a year wiser as well as a year older?' Will asked as he leaned closer to him.

'We all should be. Three wise men! I do not mind wisdom so much, but please reassure me that you have not grown sensible?'

Francis Hodgson laughed. 'Hardly. I saw Scrope Davies the other day; we spent the whole night gambling. I stumbled home to Picadilly at about two o'clock. He stayed on. The next day I went to see him. It was after lunch, and he was still in bed. Would you believe it, under his bed was a chamber pot—full to the brim—'

'With banknotes!' Will finished the anecdote with a flourish.

Byron laughed heartily: 'Good God, I can believe it!

Dear Scrope...'

'He's had a winning streak lately.'

'I hope to see him when I am next in London.'

'When will that be, George?' Will smiled.

'I shall be making my maiden speech in the House of Lords soon after my birthday.'

Francis gazed into the fire. 'What shall be your subject?'

'I am toying with the idea of the plight of the local stocking knitters. Men are starving for lack of work. They are desperate. Someone has to speak up for them.'

'Very noble of you, George, standing up for the underdog,' Francis raised his glass.

Will finished his brandy and eased himself off his chair onto the carpet. 'You don't mind if I recline at your feet do you?'

Byron reached forward and stroked Will's ash blonde hair. 'Not as long as you pour me another drink and play Ganymede to my Zeus.'

Will playfully slapped Byron's hand. 'I'm not your fag any more. You'll have me polishing your boots next! Hardly fitting behaviour for one soon to be Reverend Harness.' On his knees he reached up to the table and took the brandy decanter. He refilled Byron's glass and his own.

'If you don't mind, Reverend Harness, my glass appears to be empty also.' Francis held his tumbler out and Will poured him another measure.

'How do you amuse yourself on these long winter nights?' Will leaned against Byron's chair, resting his head on his knee.

'I have my diversions.'

'Are they pretty, these diversions of yours? I'll wager they are not di-virgins!' Francis giggled at his own joke.

Will snorted, 'Not for long they aren't.'

Byron smiled, but said nothing. They were silent for a moment.

'Do you still swim?' Francis asked. 'Hobhouse told me about you swimming the Hellespont when you were both in Greece. Christ, George, how far is that?'

'Five miles,' said Byron.

'Do you swim in the lake here?'

Byron nodded: 'In the summer; not now of course.' Will rested his head against Byron's thigh.

'Is it true that Charles Matthews drowned?'

Francis leaned forward. 'I also heard that. I always thought he was a strong swimmer.'

Byron drew a deep breath. 'He was.'

'Do you think it was suicide?' Will frowned.

Byron stroked Will's hair. 'Quite possibly. I believe he was ashamed of platonic love.'

'Not purely platonic as I understand it.' Francis swirled his brandy.

'No. But which of us can lay claim to purity in our affections?' Byron sat back in his chair and held out his glass to be refilled. Will poured him a generous measure, and met Byron's gaze.

'I think I prefer Byronic to platonic love,' he murmured.

The clock chimed eleven. Francis Hodgson yawned and stretched. He reached down and patted the dozing hound at his feet.

'Shall I show you to your bed?' Byron smiled at him.

'I think you had better. Damn tiring journey from London.'

'Are you sure you do not want to stay up for a midnight feast? We have mince pies.'

Francis considered the offer for a moment. 'No George, I'll wait until breakfast. I get dreadful indigestion if I eat this late.'

Byron stood and took a candle from the mantelpiece. 'Come on, then. Be prepared for a shock; our rooms, although comfortable, are miles apart.'

The three men made their way along the silent corridors. The snowy ground outside glowed blue in the moonlight.

'Are there spectres in your abbey?' Will peered through the gloom.

'Friendly ones, I assure you,' Byron said, 'although I have yet to see them.' He pushed open the door of a room along the passage, several yards away from the staircase leading to his own bedchamber. A bright fire illuminated the heavy drapery. Francis sat on the large bed and proceeded to pull off his boots.

'Ah, this is very grand. Suits me very well. Goodnight, George, Will.'

Will linked his arm through Byron's as they returned to the dining room. 'Let us indulge our appetites,' he whispered.

Lizzie lowered the muslin parcel into the cauldron of boiling water. She rested the wooden spoon across the rim and balanced the heavy lid on top.

Three hours: she looked at the clock. It should be cooked by twelve. If she removed it at half past eleven, she could finish it off at Joan's so it was ready after dinner. She sat down. The bells of St Mary's were pealing for Christmas morning. She sighed. Maybe she should have gone to her chapel for Mass, or at least to confession. How could she begin to explain to Père Bertrand about Byron? The priest would most probably tell her that Byron was the devil incarnate or at the very least a demon sent to tempt her, seduce her. And she had fallen. She had not resisted. Lizzie crossed herself. She closed her eyes in prayer.

'Dear mother,' she whispered, 'dear father, it did not feel like sin. He was gentle and kind. He fed me when I was hungry. He wants to ease our suffering. He gave me alms, he showed me love.' She clasped her hands tightly together. 'Love is not sinful.'

Lizzie opened her eyes. The pot over the fire had reached a vigorous boil, droplets of water splashing onto the hot coals with a sharp hiss. She poured a small amount of cold water inside to calm it a little. She took her cards from the dresser, shuffled them and cut them.

Three of Swords. A heart pierced by three blades. Three people closely connected in some kind of trouble. Surely this was herself, Byron and Robert.

La Papesse: The young woman was seated between the two pillars of wisdom and strength. She had trusted her instincts in the recent past. Did this card mean that she was right to do so?

The King of Swords: A man uneasy with power, involved with a predicament. She wondered if she would ever see Byron again.

Le Chariot: The solution to the problem was a journey, but to where? Who was to travel? Lizzie considered if it meant a literal journey or a change in her life, taking a different path.

Le Magicien: The man depicted had cards and cups on the table before him. He wielded a wand. It meant someone's ability to solve problems. In the near future resourcefulness would bring success.

L'Emperesse: Lizzie stared at the card. Seated on a throne, the woman was smiling, content. Her hands cradled her heavy, pregnant belly. Lizzie stroked her own stomach. She tried to remember when she had last had a bleeding. It had been so erratic over the summer; she had been unable to predict it. Was she already carrying Byron's child? She closed her eyes and rested her forehead on her hands.

St Mary's chimed eleven o'clock. Lizzie stood. She opened the dresser door. Inside the upper section were rows of jars. She removed one of them, opened it and inspected the contents. Would the harmless-looking herb really destroy an unborn child? Surely to kill the child would be a greater sin than to give birth outside of marriage? She replaced the lid. 'I cannot,' she said, 'I *will* not.' She placed the jar back on the shelf. Lizzie removed the pudding from the fire, wrapped it in a tea towel and placed it in her basket.

'We used the shillings you gave us to buy the goose.' Caroline Elliott grasped Lizzie's arm in excitement.

'Wait until you see it,' Michael squealed. 'It's the biggest goose in the country!'

'I don't know about that,' Joan said as she opened the door of the oven with a poker. Protecting her hands with a thick cloth, she drew out the roasting tin. She placed the bird on the table. 'I only hope it's big enough to feed all nine of us.' She sliced slivers of meat and distributed them to the eager children. She gave Lizzie one of the legs and was going to add more, but Lizzie raised her hand.

'Please, Joan, that's more than sufficient. Give the rest to your children.'

'Roast potatoes, my favourite!' Michael tucked into his dinner.

Rose slapped his hand. 'We haven't said grace yet.'

The little boy laid down his cutlery. The children put their hands together, and Lizzie joined them.

'Let us be thankful for the food we have today, Lord,' Joan led them in prayer, 'especially on Christmas Day. Let us also be thankful for the generosity of our kind friends. Amen.'

'Amen!' the children repeated. They attacked their plates with enthusiasm.

'God knows what we would have had to eat if you hadn't given us that money,' Joan said to Lizzie, 'I went to the vicar, but he said he could only give me sixpence. Sixpence, I ask you. To feed this lot.' She indicated her children with her fork. Lizzie savoured every mouthful, all the time thinking that it was not herself that should be thanked.

JANUARY 1812

*B*yron fired a parting shot at the soldiers, who by now realised they were overwhelmed if not outnumbered. He ordered his men to cease firing.

'We've done what we came to do; let's be gone!' Then he called out, 'First and Second regiment with me; Third, hold them here, then re-unite where we agreed.' He mounted his horse and the sixteen men of the First and Second followed. Triumphantly they marched toward the city, intending to meet at the Clinton Arms. The men started to sing:

> *'As Liberty lads o'er the sea*
> *Bought their freedom, and cheaply with blood,*
> *So we, boys, we*
> *Will die fighting or live free,*
> *And down with all kings but King Ludd!'*

At the top of the Derby Road their high spirits were sharply quelled. A detachment of about twenty soldiers was approaching from the opposite direction. Immediately

Byron called a halt.

'What are we to do?' Number Twelve asked. 'Should we fight?'

Byron shook his head: 'We can't take them on. There are too many of them.' He looked round at his ragged army. One of the men in the front caught his eye. 'What's to do, Captain?' he asked.

'Change of plan,' Byron called, 'The First, go left toward Mansfield; Second, branch off toward Bulwell. Number Twelve, with me. Regroup at the Inn in a few hours.'

The soldiers were approaching fast. The two groups split away; Byron and Twelve turned their horses and headed toward the Castle.

The Militia followed them, Colonel Musters calling out, 'With me, all of you!' He wasn't going to let Captain Ludd slip through his fingers. The rest of them could go hang, he thought, the prize was their leader.

'Without him they'll be finished,' he said to his Lieutenant. 'I want him alive!' he shouted. They chased down the hill, past St James' Lane. Byron spurred his horse and soon he and Twelve were at Broadmarsh, well ahead of the Militia.

'You must go now,' Byron said to Twelve, reining in his horse. 'Get yourself to the inn.'

'Captain, this is madness; they'll kill you!'

'They'll have to catch me first.'

Twelve looked at him: 'If I give myself up, they'll think I'm you.'

'Very noble, but not possible,' Byron asserted. 'I'm not having your death on my conscience.'

He took out his pistols and handed them to Twelve.

'Take these; go and let the others know I'm safe.' He removed his cloak and passed that to him also. Twelve took the pistols and cloak with reluctance. He turned his horse toward town.

'With respect, sir, you're mad.'

'I know,' said Byron.

He spurred his horse and rode away.

The colonel and his regiment reached the bottom of the hill and caught sight of their quarry as he galloped down Leen Side. 'He's undone this time,' Musters said.

Byron approached a copse of trees which provided a small amount of cover. He dismounted. It pained him, but he was going to have to leave his horse. He patted its neck. As he hurried through the trees he could hear the soldiers in the distance. He reached the bank of the river. Byron was glad that he was wearing his second best pair of riding boots as he was going to have to discard them also. He sat down and pulled them off. For a moment he stared at the ominous, dark water. An eldritch mist hovered above the surface. He prayed to Leander: The Hellespont was nothing compared to this, I'd rather swim the Styx. He waded in. Byron's cold plunge pool at Newstead was warm by comparison. He gasped, but quickly regained his composure and began to push silently through the icy River Leen.

The soldiers discovered Byron's horse.

'The captain's abandoned his mount, sir,' one of them called out, 'he can't be far away.'

They made their way along the riverbank.

'Anything?' The colonel enquired.

'There's no sign of him, sir.'

'The Blackguard can't have vanished into thin air! Keep looking.' Colonel Musters trotted up and down. He took out a small field telescope, but it was almost useless in the dark.

One of the soldiers cried out, 'Sir, I've found something!'

Musters dismounted and stalked over to him. 'What is it?' He was becoming exasperated.

'His boots, sir.' He held them up, so the colonel could

see them.

'His what??!'

The lieutenant stifled a laugh. 'Captain Ludd's boots!'

When he was certain he had swum far enough away not to be noticed, Byron hauled himself onto the riverbank. He was perished. It was utter madness. He was shivering. He needed to get indoors as soon as possible. Half jogging, he passed Hollow Stone and continued up the curfew-deserted streets towards St. Mary's. The clock chimed half past something. He stumbled along, eventually reaching the door of one of the small houses. Byron used the last ounce of his strength to hammer on the door, trying to call out a name, but he found he had lost his voice. He knocked again.

'Who is it?' a young woman asked.

He could not reply, he was coughing. The latch unbolted and Lizzie, wearing her nightgown, opened the door.

'Byron!' she exclaimed as he tumbled inside. 'Oh my sweet Lord! What's happened to you?'

She closed the door, put her pistol down on the table and led him to the hessian rug in front of the fire. He coughed. She grabbed a towel, bolted through to the bedroom and brought the blankets from Robert's empty bed. She started to dry his hair.

'I need to get out of these wet things,' he croaked. His hands shook as he tried to untie his cravat. She stripped his shirt off and helped him remove his breeches. She wrapped the soft woollen blanket around him and began to rub him down as hard as she could. His coughing turned into hoarse laughter.

'What is funny?' Lizzie raised her eyebrows.

'It's just, this evening, I have broken frames, been shot at, had a man offer to lay down his life for me, swum a river more treacherous and filthy than the Lethe and now I'm being revived by a Child of the Revolution!'

Lizzie shook her head in disbelief. He sat down in the chair at the fireside. 'I owe you so much,' he said.

Lizzie removed his stockings, which were ruined, and towelled his feet dry. She took a warm tea towel, which had aired in front of the fire and wrapped his feet in it, and then she rested them on a footstool. She draped his breeches over the other fireside chair. 'I'll make you some tea,' she said.

'Do you have anything stronger?'

Lizzie shook her head. 'I'm afraid not. No Portugese wine here, I'm sorry.'

Byron laughed: 'Then tea will have to do, Miss Molyneux.'

She put the kettle on to boil. A thought occurred to her. 'There's no chance you could be followed here?'

He shook his head. 'I lost them at the Leen.'

Lizzie looked down at his feet. 'Where are your boots?'

'I left them by the river. If I'd kept them on, they would have pulled me down to a watery grave.'

Lizzie crossed herself. 'God forbid,' she said.

There was a sharp knock at the door. Lizzie's heart leapt to her mouth. Byron put his finger to his lips. He looked over at the door. Lizzie pointed to the bedroom. He scuttled through from the kitchen. Lizzie picked up her pistol from the table and cocked it. Then she placed her left hand on the latch of the door. 'Who is it?'

'His Majesty's Militia, Madam. Open up!'

She unlocked the door, holding the pistol out of sight. A young soldier stood outside.

'Beg your pardon, Miss,' he said, 'but we're searching for known frame breakers. Most particularly, the leader, calls himself Captain Ludd. Have you seen or heard anything or anyone suspicious tonight?'

'No one,' Lizzie said.

In the bedroom, Byron failed to stifle his coughing.

'Are you alone, Miss?'

'No,' she said, 'The other person who lives here is my brother.'

'Where is he?' asked the soldier.

'He's in bed, sir; he's not well.'

'I'll not trouble you any further. Don't answer the door to anyone else. There are dangerous men about.'

'I understand.' Lizzie was relieved that he wasn't going to search the house.

'Goodnight, Miss.' The soldier bowed stiffly and was gone.

She locked the door. Sighing with relief, Lizzie made the pistol safe and laid it on the table. She took the steaming kettle from the fire. Byron, still wrapped in the blanket, leaned round the bedroom door. 'Are you alright?' he asked.

Lizzie nodded. He returned to the kitchen; he had draped the blanket round himself like a Roman Toga, or a Highland cloak.

'You should be on the stage,' Byron said. 'I half believed I was your brother.'

'One brother in prison is quite enough for me,' Lizzie said, pouring the tea. She added a generous spoonful of honey. They sat down at the table. He looked at the gun.

'I'm glad you are making use of your pistol.'

She passed Byron a tea cup. 'What are you going to do now?' she asked.

'I'll have to stay here, at least for tonight.'

Lizzie's eyes met his gaze. 'I wasn't sure if I'd ever see you again,' she murmured.

'I fully intended to meet with you,' he said, sipping his tea, 'although not in these circumstances. Tomorrow, if I'm not back at Newstead by noon, Fletcher knows to send the carriage to the Clinton Arms to collect me, whether I'm alive, or otherwise. I will be needing some stockings and a pair of boots...'

'You can borrow Robert's spares,' suggested Lizzie. 'There are plenty of stockings, but I don't know if the boots will fit you.'

'My feet are usually smaller than everyone else's,' he said. 'I'm sure we can make them fit.'

He took her hand and kissed it. 'You are my saviour.' Byron finished his tea and rubbed his eyes.

'I'm exhausted,' he yawned, 'let's go to bed.' Then he grinned. 'I don't usually say those two phrases together!' They both laughed.

Lizzie took the candle from the table and led him to the bedroom. 'I'm afraid my bed isn't as big as yours,' she said, 'and the room is rather cold.'

'No matter. We'll be cozy in a small bed.' He climbed in beside her.

She blew out the candle and pulled the bedclothes over them. Byron rested his head on her shoulder. Lizzie stroked his hair and kissed his forehead. She was relieved that he had ceased coughing.

'You remind me of Augusta, my sister,' he whispered.

'Where is your sister?' Lizzie asked.

'She lives near Cambridge with her horse-mad husband. I haven't seen her in ages.'

'Would you like to see her again?'

'Yes.' Byron's eyes were heavy. 'I would like that very much.'

Soon he was sound asleep.

Byron opened his eyes. His face was covered by a linen sheet. 'Is this a shroud?' he whispered, 'did I die in the river last night?' There was no reply, he was alone. He yawned. 'Does one yawn when dead?' He could hear someone moving around in the next room. A drawer opening, the rattle of cutlery. He pushed back the sheets and sat up. The pale sun illuminated Lizzie's possessions on the bedside table. Her comb and hairbrush were next to one of the smallest Bibles he had ever seen. Her rosary was resting on the Bible. He sighed with relief, remembering where he was. The latch on the bedroom door moved and Lizzie entered.

'You do realize, this is impossibly early for me,' Byron said with a jovial smile.

Lizzie laughed.

'I'm glad to see you laugh, Lizzie.' As he stood up, Lizzie's expression changed; her mouth dropped open.

'Do not feign shock, my dear. You have seen me naked before.' He gestured, spreading his arms wide, like a heroic actor about to give a speech. 'What am I going to wear? Are my breeches dry?'

'Almost,' Lizzie said, trying not to gawp at him, 'but your shirt is beyond repair.'

'Ah, yes. Silk does not like the River Leen.'

Lizzie opened a drawer on the chest next to Robert's bed. 'You can wear one of Robert's.' She drew out a plain cambric shirt. She helped Byron slip his arms into it and arranged it on his shoulders. He began to chuckle. His wrists and hands extended far beyond the cuffs.

'Oh dear,' Byron laughed. 'My feet are small, but my arms are, I believe, made for swimming.' He took it off. Lizzie sighed. Then a thought occurred to her.

'My father left a couple of shirts here. He was a taller man, or *is* a taller man, if he's still alive.' She brought one out and Byron slipped it on.

'Much better.' He buttoned it up. 'Where is your father?'

'He left about three years ago. He sailed from Liverpool to a French colony in the Americas. He always said he would send for us. Robert and I were working the frames by then.' She paused. 'We have heard nothing.'

'Why did he go there?'

'I believe we have some relatives in New Orleans. I don't even know if he arrived safely.'

'So we have both lost our parents.' Byron's voice was kind. He enfolded her in his arms once more.

'I had hoped to receive a letter from him, but I gave up

that hope long ago.'

Byron held her tightly. He kissed her forehead. She raised her eyes. She kissed him, cherishing his presence, but wondering how long it would be before he left, or was taken away from her.

'I am used to being alone,' Lizzie said.

She disappeared into the kitchen and returned with Byron's breeches.

'These are dry now.' She put them on the bed and held out a pair of silk stockings. 'I have plenty of these. They are new.'

Byron examined them. 'They are very high quality. Did you make them?'

Lizzie nodded. 'On the old frame. You have to knit them all in one. Now anyone can run the cheaper ones up and seam them. We call those, Spider Work.'

He sat down on the bed and slid them over his feet. Then he drew up his breeches, stood and buttoned the fly.

'Would you like some breakfast?' Lizzie asked.

Byron nodded. 'What are you going to make for us?'

'Frumenty. I hope that's acceptable?'

'How delightful!' Byron smiled. 'I haven't eaten porridge since I was a child.'

Lizzie took Robert's boots from beside the bed. She passed them to Byron.

'Try these first.'

He pulled them on and paced the room a little. 'I think these will be perfect, with an extra pair of stockings.' Lizzie fetched some for him. Once he had them on, he replaced the boots, stamped his feet and walked a few steps. 'I wouldn't be able to play Cricket in them, but they are comfortable enough. Thank you, Lizzie.' He kissed her. 'How do I look?'

She stepped back and admired him. He could pass for a frameknitter, except for his face, which would make him remarkable to even the most unobservant person. 'You'll do.'

He pretended to scold her: 'Such impertinence! Now go and make my breakfast!'

Lizzie imitated a curtsey. 'Yes m'lud,' she smiled.

As Lizzie cleared away the dishes Byron stood and stepped over to the mantelpiece. He lifted up a miniature portrait depicting a man with long hair tied in a ponytail and his high jacket collar and ruffled shirt in the fashion from the end of the previous century. Lizzie noticed Byron examining it.

'That's Papa. When he was much younger. We used to have a portrait of *Maman* too, but he took it with him when he went abroad.'

'He's handsome. I can see a resemblance.'

'Papa always said that Robert and I had his eyes, but our mother's smile.'

'I didn't go to my mother's funeral,' Byron confessed. 'I regret that. I do not enjoy saying goodbye to anyone. I don't even like to say goodnight. Maybe it's a superstition; it's so final, as though you're never going to meet again.' Byron sighed.

He replaced the portrait on the mantelpiece. He looked thoughtful.

'Your brother resembles you, I take it?'

'Yes.'

'And he is a similar height? I can see from his shirt he is not a large man.'

Lizzie nodded. 'When we were children, we used to dress in each other's clothes for fun, to trick people.' She smiled, remembering.

Byron's face showed the raven expression once again. His eyes were bright.

'Say that again,' he said.

'People couldn't tell us apart. We used to swap our clothes.'

St Mary's chimed nine o'clock. There was a rap at the door.

'*Mon Dieu*! I forgot the time,' Lizzie whispered, 'it's Mr Jackson.'

'Who is he?' Byron hissed.

'The factor. He's come to collect my stockings and pay me.'

'He doesn't know me from Adam,' Byron whispered. 'Tell him I'm your cousin, just up from London.'

Lizzie opened the door. Thomas Jackson bustled in. His face was red from the cold. He put down his bag and rubbed his hands together.

'Blimey, Liz, you took your time!' He noticed Byron. 'Are you entertaining?!'

'Good morning, sir!' Byron said as he put out his hand. 'George Gordon.'

Jackson shook his hand. 'Thomas Jackson, Hosier.'

'George is my cousin, Mr Jackson. He's just returned from London.'

'Indeed, sir? And what is your trade?'

'Imports, exports... Mainly textiles.'

'You mean abroad?' Jackson was impressed.

'Indeed I do. I trade throughout the world. Lizzie was just showing me the fine stockings she has made. I expect you are extremely proud of them?'

Jackson scratched his hairless head. 'Yes, they are fine quality.'

'Indeed!' Byron picked up a pair from the bench near the frame. 'They would grace the leg of any dandy gentleman in London.' He exchanged a glance with Lizzie. She gnawed her lip for fear of giving him away. She had to look away to stop herself from exploding with laughter.

'I wouldn't know much about dandies. But, they are fine, I'll grant you that.'

'And they make you a fine profit, I'll warrant.'

Mr Jackson shifted from one foot to the other. 'These days you're lucky to get owt for owt. Still, they are one of the more profitable goods. Can't shift them in any quantity, but when they do sell, they make a tidy sum.'

'And of course you pay a higher rate for top quality work by such a skilled stockinger?'

'She gets the going rate.'

'What is the going rate?' Byron fixed Jackson in his gaze.

'Two shillings a week.'

Byron blinked. 'How much do you pay the workshop frameknitters?'

Jackson drew his breath slowly. Lizzie wondered if he looked embarrassed. 'They get three shillings.'

'Because they're men, and because they make cheap, plentiful goods that don't take skill or talent to produce.' Lizzie could see that Byron was incensed, but he controlled his voice.

Jackson nodded.

Byron leaned forward on the table: 'You've already admitted that Lizzie's work fetches a higher price. And it's also of a higher quality, so surely it deserves a greater reward...'

Jackson was silent.

'Or at the very least, the same payment that her fellow workers get?' Byron stared Jackson down. Lizzie looked from one to the other. 'Mr Jackson, you will certainly earn greater respect from society at large for your foresight and philanthropism,' said Byron, 'and in these troubled times appearances are everything.'

'I can see what you mean, sir.' Yet Jackson looked suspicious. Lizzie was afraid that he wouldn't believe that this eloquent stranger was her cousin. Byron put out his hand. 'Well, that comes of bartering in the capital. Do we have an agreement, sir?'

Jackson shook Byron's hand, though his expression remained wary. 'Very well, Mr Gordon. Three shillings it is.' He looked at Lizzie. 'I had no idea you had such *influential* relatives, Liz!' He gave a hoarse laugh. Lizzie's hands were shaking a little as she collected the paired stockings and helped Jackson load them into his bag. He began counting out coins on the table.

'Starting from today, naturally,' Byron coerced.

'Naturally...' Jackson added the third shilling. 'Well, goodbye Mr Gordon. See you the same time next week, Liz.' He left, whistling through his teeth.

Lizzie closed the door. She turned slowly towards Byron.

'Has that repaid my stumbling into your house soaking wet in the middle of the night?' he asked.

'More than repaid!' She kissed him and looked away. Her expression was troubled.

'What is wrong?' he asked.

'I don't want to seem ungrateful,' she began, 'but you may have done more harm than good.'

Byron frowned. 'How is that? I don't understand. How can you possibly live for a week on two shillings? A London moll would earn more in one night.'

Lizzie counted the coins. 'You don't know what it's like. I'll be branded as a trouble maker.' He could see fear in her eyes. 'And I don't think he believed that you are my cousin.'

'Lizzie, the last thing I wanted was to upset you, or put you in jeopardy.' He sat down.

'I know you can't pretend to be someone that you are not.'

'I always thought I was a good actor.'

'On the stage perhaps, but this is real life. Here you are speaking your own words, not those of a character.'

Byron looked up at her. 'My own words,' he said. He placed his hands on her shoulders. 'You are my inspiration, Lizzie, and I will use my words to fight for you.'

'Will you write another poem?'

'Better than that...' His expression was determined. 'When I make my speech to the House of Lords, I shall tell them of the misery and injustice I see all around me. I shall make them see how you are suffering, all of you. If I can't pretend to be one of you, the very least I can do is to use my position and privilege to help you.'

Lizzie smiled at his resolve.

'Come with me to Newstead,' he said abruptly.

Lizzie's eyes widened. 'I can't just disappear,' she said.

'Why not? You'll be safe there. I can't bear to think of you here alone at night. Please! You can help me write my speech.'

Lizzie laughed. He was so impetuous. 'I'm afraid that one day your *fougue* will get you into a lot of trouble,' she said.

'Quite possibly. But you haven't said yes.' He looked into her eyes. She couldn't resist him.

'Very well.'

'You will? You're saying yes?'

'Yes, Byron. But I can't stay there forever.'

'And I must go to London to make the speech. And once *Childe Harold* is published I suppose I'll have to live in London for a while. But you could stay with me there as well.'

Lizzie was enraptured by the wildness in his eyes but her better judgment prevailed. 'I'll stay with you at Newstead for a few days,' she said. 'But then I must return to do my work. I can't expect you to support me. And I don't want to be one of your servants.'

'I understand. You are fiercely independent. What's more, you're used to being alone. And you certainly don't need a man to order you about. Is that it?'

Lizzie nodded.

'I'll compromise with you, ' he bargained. 'Come to Newstead for the time being.' He took her hand. 'We'll hatch our plot together. We shall take on the tyrants and free your brother. Only then shall I release you.'

Lizzie smiled at his audacity and his certainty; he made it sound so easy. 'Alright,' she said. He kissed her again.

'I love having you with me,' he said.

St Mary's chimed half past nine.

'We have at least two and a half hours before we need

to go to the inn,' murmured Byron between kisses. He began to unbutton his shirt.

'You've only just got dressed!' Lizzie gasped.

'Well, you can dress me again, later,' he said, ' and then I'll tell you my other plan.'

'What other plan?' she asked as he led her to the bedroom.

Byron sat down on her bed. 'My secret plan,' he grunted as he pulled off one boot, 'which, if executed with precision will bring about a satisfactory conclusion to the present and rather pressing situation.' He drew her down beside him and began to unlace her dress. 'Which is exactly what I am about to do now.'

Byron helped Lizzie descend the carriage steps. Their arrival was greeted by two small boys that appeared from the side of the Abbey. Lizzie guessed that the boys were brothers, the elder aged ten or eleven. He was wearing an apron, which like his hands was black with polish. The lads scooted to the main entrance and lined up at the bottom of the steps like two miniature soldiers on parade, ready to be inspected by their master.

'They're Fletcher's boys,' Byron explained with a smile. 'I'm not *quite* old enough to be their father.'

They approached the steps.

'Good afternoon m'lord,' the boys chorused.

'Good afternoon. What have you been up to today, Fletcher Minor?'

The younger of the two stepped forward. 'I've been digging potatoes and cutting sprouts, m'lord.'

'Excellent! We'll be having some of those for dinner, I expect.' Then he addressed the other boy: 'Fletcher Major, I trust that you have been behaving yourself?'

'Yes, m'lord,' he said as he held out his blackened hands. 'I've been helping Papa polish your boots, m'lord.'

'And I'm sure you have made an excellent job of it!' Byron smiled and took two coins from his pocket. 'Here you are.' The boys held out their hands and Byron tossed the coins to them individually. He indicated Lizzie: 'This lady is Miss Molyneux. She is my guest.'

The two lads bowed politely. 'Pleased to make your acquaintance, Miss,' ventured the senior of the brothers, holding his dirty hands behind his back.

'Don't they have wonderful manners?' Byron nodded to Lizzie, 'That comes from Mr Fletcher being educated.' He turned to the lads once more. 'Does your father still read the newspaper to you?'

'Yes, m'lord. Every evening.'

'And what do you want to be when you are a grown man?'

'A gentleman's valet, if you please m'lord.'

Byron hummed agreement. 'And what about you?' He turned to the smaller boy.

'A Luddite!' he exclaimed.

Lizzie exchanged a look with Byron.

'Do you indeed? And why would you want to be one of those?' Byron raised an eyebrow.

The little boy shrugged.

'Don't you know?'

The lad shook his head.

'Last week I recall you wanted to be a race horse,' Byron reminded him. 'I think that would be safer.'

Byron brought out his pocket watch. 'Three o'clock: time for your tea.'

The boys nodded.

'Off you go.' The boys skedaddled around the building toward the kitchen. Byron shouted after them: 'Make sure you wash your hands properly!'

He turned to Lizzie: 'That's what comes of reading the press, I suppose. Imagine it, an eight-year-old wanting to be a Luddite...' He shook his head. 'Mind you, there are worse things...' They ascended the steps. 'At least he doesn't want to be a soldier, or a butcher.'

'He's fortunate to have the choice,' Lizzie remarked as

she followed Byron inside.

Wolf greeted them as they made their way through the Great Hall, the dog's tail waving frantically from side to side and its claws pattering over the wooden floor. Byron stroked its head. He seemed pre-occupied. He spoke to Lizzie, or to no one in particular. 'Dogs are always pleased to see you. No matter what mood you are in, or how long you've been away. So much more trustworthy than people...'

They proceeded into the dining room and almost immediately Fletcher brought a tea tray to them. 'If I may say so, m'lord, I'm glad to see you back safely.' He began to pour the tea.

'Thank you, Fletcher. If it hadn't been for Miss Molyneux, I would not be here now.' Byron took his seat at the head of the table.

'Did you know that Georgie wants to be a frame-breaker?' he asked, as he casually helped himself to a slice of bread and butter. Fletcher passed a teacup to Lizzie, almost slopping it.

'No, m'lord, I did not. I'll have words with him.'

'No need for that. I quite like the idea of you breeding rebels,' Byron smirked. 'Just as long as you don't start a revolution in the kitchen and poison me.'

Despite the fact that Byron was wearing her father's old shirt and her brother's boots, he was still an aristocrat, someone who was used to giving orders, and used to being obeyed; yet somehow uneasy with the role. Was there a flicker of fear in his eyes? Fear that he might one day become the focus of derision or even hatred: Did he prefer to be on the side of the oppressed, rather than being mistaken for an oppressor, simply because of his position in society? Lizzie's father had told her about the Terror, how he had narrowly escaped being a victim of the guillotine. How easily the revolt of the downtrodden people had transformed into a witch-hunt; executing anyone who had been associated with the ruling class.

'Would you prefer cake, or bread and butter, Lizzie?' Byron's voice broke into her reverie. She stared at the rich fruit cake and the delicate slices of fine white bread.

'Cake please.' Fletcher cut her a slice.

'We can manage on our own now, Fletcher.' Byron dismissed him with a wave of his hand. He munched mouthfuls of cake. 'After tea you can unpack your things.' He noticed Lizzie's serious expression. 'Are you thinking about your brother?' Byron finished his cake and started on the bread and butter; they had eaten no lunch, after all.

Lizzie nodded. 'This morning you said that you had a secret plan to get him out of the gaol.'

Byron smiled. He gulped his tea to wash down the bread. 'Yes, and it involves a masquerade.' He tapped his fingers on the table and leaned forward. His voice was almost a whisper, despite them being alone in the room. 'We will go to the prison, I will be in disguise. I shall pretend to be a monk who has come to hear your brother's confession. Once inside, we will dress Robert in some of your clothes and the guards will think that he is you.'

Lizzie tried to imagine it. 'But the guards will see two of me, surely.'

Byron nodded. 'There's the stumbling block. We have to distract them somehow, so that they only see 'you' once.' He paused. 'Can you think of anyone who would be able to do that? Distract a man to help Robert? Is there someone who would want him freed as much as you or I?'

Lizzie thought for a moment: 'Sarah.'

'Sarah?'

'A girl with whom Robert is in love... I believe she could do it. She does care for him, and she can get a man's attention.'

'Can she be trusted?'

Lizzie nodded: 'I think so.'

'Where would we find her?' Byron poured another cup of tea.

'She lodges at the Angel tavern.'

Byron's eyes lit up with recognition: '*That* Sarah!' he laughed.

'You know her?'

'In a manner of speaking...' He sipped his tea. Lizzie looked down at her plate. She blushed as she imagined Byron in bed with Sarah. Byron took her hand. 'My dear, you are not the only object of my affections. Please don't be jealous, it's most unbecoming.'

Lizzie was angry with herself. Why was she concerned about Byron going with Sarah? She hadn't felt like this when she met his maid Susan, and she had certainly shared his bed. Maybe it was because Byron had now been in her house and bed.

'Lizzie, you are very special to me,' he said as he looked into her eyes. 'Surely you can't doubt that?' He bit his lip. 'Do you want me to tell you that I love you?'

Lizzie blinked away a shameful tear. She shook her head.

'For the first time since I met you, I do not believe you,' he said. He sighed as he lifted Lizzie out of her seat. He enfolded her in his arms as she sobbed. He stroked her hair.

'Oh, my dear. I believe that Sarah will be willing to help us. She is a very generous girl. However, she does *not* love me, and I do *not* love her. And I promise that we will succeed in rescuing your brother.'

Lizzie looked up at him. She wanted to tell him that she loved him, but at the same time she did not want him to know. She swallowed the words. 'I'm sorry,' she said as she wiped her eyes, 'it's just that I'm so worried about Robert. You are our only hope.'

Byron drew a deep breath. 'I take my responsibilities seriously.' He kissed her again. After a moment, he picked up her bag and gestured to her to follow him.

'Come on, you can unpack your things in my bedchamber. Then, after dinner, I'll make a start on my speech.'

Fletcher handed Byron the newspaper. 'I thought you'd want to read this, m'lord. I kept it for you from yesterday.'

'Thank you, Fletcher.'

Byron placed the paper on the table next to his plate and began reading, tucking into a large portion of bubble and squeak at the same time. Fletcher refilled the wineglasses and stood back. Lizzie noticed Byron's expression change as he read. He was enraged. He dropped his fork onto his plate with a clatter.

'Damn him!'

Lizzie flinched and the candle flames quivered. Byron was furious. He snatched up the newspaper.

'That pig-eyed monstrosity that calls himself Regent, do you see what he's done?' He showed her the article. She scanned it and read out loud: 'The Prince has ordered a reward of fifty pounds for information leading to the apprehension and conviction of frame breakers. What would that be to you, four or five years' wages?'

Lizzie nodded: 'Easily.'

'The dough-faced sack of lard thinks he can bribe you into betraying your fellows.' Byron shook his head. 'It proves he's afraid.' He jabbed the air with his knife. 'It proves that the authorities are running out of ideas.' He poured gravy over his potatoes and resumed eating. 'They can't appeal to us on a moral ground, for they are in the wrong, and they know it. So they think they can barter with blood money.'

Byron continued: 'If the death penalty is brought in, the frame breakers will be sent to the gallows. A man's life worth less than a machine!'

He fixed her gaze with his glowering eyes. 'This is a declaration of war on the working people of this country.'

Byron gulped his wine. 'Would they erect a gibbet on every field? Hang up men like scarecrows? I tell you something Lizzie, it will drive already desperate men into the forest and it will become a den of outlaws once more. When men have nothing left to lose, and death may be a relief, then they are truly dangerous.'

Lizzie sipped her wine. He finished eating. He stood up and took the wine bottle from Fletcher. Byron picked up his glass and refilled it. The clock chimed seven.

'I am going to write upstairs. Please join me, when you have finished your supper.'

Byron moved to the other end of the room. Fletcher took a small candle from the mantelpiece and in silence lit his master's way for him.

Lizzie took up the paper once more. She read about an Earl who had declared himself bankrupt during his divorce in order to prevent his wife from gaining any financial benefit. Lizzie knew all too well what would probably happen to the unfortunate woman. She was glad that she had at least a little income of her own. Lizzie shivered a little and stood up. She had a bizarre feeling that she was being watched. Crossing herself, she looked around, but there was no one. She picked up her wine glass and ascended the silent stairs to Byron's bedroom.

Tapped on the door, Lizzie received no answer. She let herself in. Byron was writing rapidly at the desk, where only a few weeks before she had read her cards. He did not look up or acknowledge her. He was utterly engrossed. She silently closed the door behind her and moved closer to him. He glanced up at her, his expression one of terror.

'Jesus, you frightened me!' he exclaimed.

'I'm sorry,' said Lizzie, 'I did knock.'

'I honestly did not hear you. I thought you were the White Lady.'

'Who is she?'

'She's supposed to haunt the Abbey. I've never seen her, until now.'

'I'm not a spirit,' Lizzie reassured him. She placed her hand on his shoulder and sat next to him. 'I'm real.'

He smiled. 'Yes, you are.' He kissed her.

'Are you writing your speech?' Lizzie looked at his papers.

'I am. It will be my maiden speech, the first time that I have addressed the House of Lords.'

'Are you nervous?' asked Lizzie.

'I suppose I will be. I must think of it in the same way as going on stage. The only difference being that I shan't be playing a character. I shall be myself.'

'May I read it?'

'I'll read it to you tomorrow, and you can help me with some of the finer details; make sure that I have described your plight accurately, so that there is no room for misunderstanding.'

Lizzie finished her wine, and Byron poured her the last of the bottle. She yawned.

'You are ready to go to bed, I think.'

She nodded.

'I'll join you once this is finished,' he said, and resumed writing.

Lizzie unlaced and removed her dress. She placed her shoes under a chair. Without looking up Byron said: 'Leave your stockings on; I prefer it.'

Lizzie looked at his beautiful face, which was motionless as he concentrated on his writing. She climbed into his bed and nestled among the soft pillows and warm blankets. The wind was buffeting against the window. She felt safe. The last thing she heard before she fell asleep was the scratching of his pen on the paper.

My Nereid, come to me in the cloister. I will show you how to master the waves.

Lizzie found the cryptic note on the bed beside her. Byron was nowhere to be seen. As she dressed she remembered falling asleep, and then being woken by him, in the dead of night. She was unsure if their lovemaking had been a dream. She wrapped her shawl about her shoulders and hurried down the stairs to the cloisters.

A second paper was placed conspicuously in her path, on the bottom step.

Follow me to the water.

An arrow pointed the direction. As Lizzie passed the cloister windows she noticed that the overgrown herb garden was bathed in winter sunshine. Hoar frost glistened on the bare branches of the straggly shrubs. She could hear the sound of water being disturbed along the corridor. She saw a pile of clothes on the floor near a doorway. The opening in the wall exposed a room, its floor well below the level of the cloister; it was like a wine cellar, devoid of bottles. A flight of stone steps led downwards. Byron was swimming through the cold water, which was deep and filled the room. Lizzie watched as he pushed his way along easily, completely at home and comfortable. He was in his element.

He turned at the end and called out to her. 'Good morning!' He drew himself toward the steps. 'Why don't you get in?' he asked.

Lizzie shivered. 'It's too cold.'

'Once you're in the water, you will feel warmer, I promise,' he said.

Lizzie looked unconvinced.

'If you jump in, you will not notice the cold.' Byron frowned. 'Can you swim?'

Lizzie shook her head. 'I don't think so. I have never tried.'

'Don't worry,' he said, 'I'll teach you.' He trod the water, gazing up at her. He extended his arm, beckoning. 'Come on: baptism by full immersion.'

She reached out to him.

'You had better take off your clothes.'

Lizzie undressed and cautiously stepped down. She

crouched on the step closest to the surface. Byron took her hand. He pulled her in. She shrieked as the cold water enveloped her. She panicked. Her legs thrashed.

'I've got you...' He held her tightly. 'If you relax, you'll float,' he said as he supported her. 'Look at the sunshine.'

Lizzie tilted her head back and saw the sunlight dappling the ceiling with reflections of the water. 'There, you see?' She stopped moving and began to sink. She frantically kicked. Byron lifted her up.

'Don't kick your legs too hard, push outwards.' She did so. He released her and her arms paddled in front of her. 'The same with your arms, push the water away,' he demonstrated.

Lizzie copied him, managing to stay in one place for a moment. Byron shook the water from his dark hair. 'Watch,' he said. Tumbling backwards into the water, he dived right to the bottom of the pool. Then he returned to the surface. He grinned as he reappeared in front of Lizzie. She started to sink once more and he lifted her up.

'You are like a mermaid,' she said.

'Well, a mer-man, if there is such a creature. A son of Poseidon!' He dived again to the bottom, and this time he swam the length of the room underwater. Lizzie turned and watched him resurface near the steps. 'Come to me,' he said.

She pulled her arms forward and propelled herself along. Her legs kicked outwards and she felt a moment of natural buoyancy. She was no longer cold.

'That's it,' said Byron, 'you are swimming.'

When she reached him, he caught her and prevented her from sinking. She found a hold on the steps. Byron turned round in the water and faced the doorway. 'Fletcher!' he shouted. His voice echoed against the stone. His servant appeared.

'Fetch towels for us both.'

Lizzie tried to hide behind Byron. Fletcher nodded: 'Of course, m'lord.' Lizzie could see him looking at her.

'When you have finished gawping at Miss Molyneux, if you please...' Fletcher looked embarrassed. He offered a short bow and left them. Byron laughed.

'Let's swim to the end and back before he brings the towels. I'll race you!'

Lizzie hoped that if she kept moving she wouldn't sink. Byron plunged forward and glided easily to the opposite wall. Lizzie pushed away from the steps and drew herself over to him. 'You win,' she gasped as she reached the end. He caught her. 'I'd drown if I was on my own,' she said.

'Hold onto my shoulders and I'll carry you along.'

Lizzie rested her chin on his back. He swam in a more leisurely fashion to the steps then heaved himself out and took the towels from Fletcher. 'That will be all for now,' Byron said. He helped Lizzie find her footing then draped one of the towels around her and began to rub her dry.

'I think everyone should be able to swim,' he said and kissed her. 'Let's have some breakfast: baklava pastries today.' He began to dress. 'Then, afterwards, I'll read you my speech.'

By the time they had finished eating, the sky was clouding over. The trees bowed in the wind and the surface of the lake broke into uneasy crests and troughs. An eerie light coloured the clouds yellow. Byron looked out the dining room window.

'The weather has turned on us.' He picked up his papers from the other end of the table.

'Did you write the entire speech last night?' Lizzie asked.

'Most of it,' Byron nodded. 'I need you to help me, though. There are a few details I must check with you; it must be wholly accurate.'

A mixture of snow and rain pelted the window.

'I wondered how long it would be before our Sunday turned into a snow day,' he said.

Lizzie had forgotten that it was Sunday. She had missed

going to Mass, again. Byron noticed her troubled expression.

'What is it?' he asked.

'I haven't been to Mass in weeks.'

'Are you afraid that your God will be angry with you?' He sounded almost flippant. She nodded. There was a curl on his lip and a hint of pity in his eyes.

'Are you mocking me?' she asked.

'Not at all,' he said. 'If you truly believe that an unjust deity will send you to hell for missing a few services, then you must make amends.' He stroked the hair away from her forehead.

'Personally, I don't believe that any god would treat someone so valuable with such contempt. If you still believe in sin, Lizzie, your sins are far less significant than the machinations of the powerful men of this world. If there is such a judgmental being, it surely has bigger fish to fry than you, my dear.'

Lizzie regarded at him: 'If?' she said.

Byron smiled. 'Yes, if... I have no proof one way or the other. And neither have you.'

'Are you not afraid of hell?'

'Men make their own hell, here on earth. They wage wars, they rape, they murder, and they starve and oppress each other. They make up stories to frighten people into submission. Our lives are short,' he said, 'but they need not be miserable.' In the strange winter light his face looked even more pale and unearthly.

'Then what is the purpose of our lives?' Lizzie's voice was a whisper.

'The object of life is sensation. I am on the side of Epicurus.'

Lizzie looked confused.

Byron leaned forward: 'I do not believe that we were put on this earth to suffer. We should seek out pleasure and enjoyment. If it was good enough for the ancient Greeks, who lived long before your saviour, then it is good enough for me.'

'Do you believe then, that Catholics are wrong?'

Byron was silent for a moment. Then he said, 'I believe that you should be allowed to hold and practise whatever faith you like. I may not agree with what you believe, but I will defend your right to do so. I apply the same to Anglicans, Hindus, Hebrews, Arabs and Atheists.'

'Are you an Atheist?' Lizzie was afraid that he believed in nothing.

'As I have said already, I have no proof one way or the other. That is not the same thing.'

He took her hand. 'If it would make you feel better, we can go to the chapel. This house was an Abbey before King Henry's vandals ransacked it.' He picked up his papers and led her down the corridor. They returned to the cloisters. The sleet had turned to snow and there was already a light covering clinging to the shrubs in the courtyard.

Byron showed Lizzie into the chapel. Candles were burning on the altar. Did it matter that this chapel now belonged to the English church? How could she confess with no priest to hear her? She crossed herself. She drew out her rosary and knelt. Lizzie closed her eyes. She prayed for herself and for Byron, that their carnal sin might be forgiven. She prayed for Robert, that he might be spared any further suffering and that he would escape the gallows. Would her prayer be answered? If what Byron said were true, it might all be folly. She could feel him looking at her. She opened her eyes. Lizzie stood and turned to face him. He was smiling. He held out his hand and she took it.

'If I read my speech to you now, there will be time to correct it before lunch,' he said.

They ascended the stairs once more and arrived at the Long Gallery. Snow pattered on the window panes. Byron stood at one end and gestured for Lizzie to be seated at the other end.

'I need to make sure that you can hear me from there.

The House of Lords is a large chamber. No good will come of the most eloquent speech if it cannot be heard.'

He cleared his throat: 'My Lords—' he began. At that moment his dog padded into the room. Byron paused. 'I suppose there might be latecomers,' he said. Wolf sat next to Lizzie. She patted him and he looked expectantly at his master.

Byron resumed: 'The subject now submitted to your lordships for the first time, though new to the House, is by no means new to the country. I believe it has occupied the serious thoughts of all descriptions of persons. As a person in some degree connected with the suffering county, though a stranger not only to this House in general, but to almost every individual whose attention I presume to solicit, I must claim some of your lordships' indulgence, whilst I offer a few observations on a question in which I consider myself deeply interested.'

He looked at Lizzie. She nodded. His voice was loud and clear, his emphasis sincere and passionate.

He continued: 'During the short time I passed in Nottinghamshire, not twelve hours elapsed without some fresh act of violence. But whilst these outrages must be admitted to exist to an alarming extent, it cannot be denied that they have arisen from circumstances of the most unparalleled distress. The perseverance of these miserable men in their proceedings tends to prove that nothing but absolute want could have driven a large, and once honest and industrious body of the people, into the commission of excesses so hazardous to themselves, their families and the community.'

He paused and addressed Lizzie personally. 'This is the part where I must ask you for help.'

He continued: 'By the adoption of one species of frame in particular, one man performed the work of many, and the superfluous labourers were thrown out of employment. Yet it is to be observed, that the work thus executed was inferior in quality; not marketable at home, and merely hurried over with a view to exportation. It was called in the cant of the trade, Spider Work'

He paused and looked at Lizzie. 'Is that correct?'

'Yes,' she said. 'Spider Work.'

As Byron described the framebreaking and the way that the militia had been brought in to quell it, Lizzie thought of Robert. She remembered the demonstration in the market square, the crowd being surrounded. She could hear the anger in Byron's voice:

'You call these men a mob, desperate, dangerous and ignorant. Are we aware of our obligations to a mob? It is the mob that labour in your fields, and serve in your houses, that man your navy, and recruit your army, that have enabled you to defy the world and can also defy you when neglect and calamity have driven them to despair. You may call the people a mob, but do not forget that the mob too often speaks the sentiments of the people!'

Lizzie stood up. She applauded him. Wolf barked. Byron was flushed with pride.

'Do you think it is acceptable?'

'Passionate and dramatic,' Lizzie said. 'I don't think they'll like it though.'

'No, neither do I.' He smiled ruefully. 'They will not be such a receptive audience.' He patted Wolf. Fletcher entered the room.

'My Lord, lunch is ready.'

Byron smiled. 'Thank goodness.' He started to make his way to the dining room. 'We cannot begin a revolution on empty stomachs.'

'Bless you, my child,' Byron said as he made the sign of the cross. He pulled the monk's cowl over his head so that it concealed his hair. 'I absolve you of all your sins. Both those you have committed and those you have yet to commit.' He drew his hands together in a mockery of prayer. 'Am I pious enough for you?' The dwindling afternoon sunshine sparkled on the frosted window panes.

As Lizzie sat on a window seat, her stomach churned a little. She wondered if she had eaten too much. Byron pulled a second robe from the open blanket box. 'I had a few of these robes made for a party last year,' he chuckled, remembering the less than holy masquerade.

'This is not a party game, it is serious.' Lizzie was aware that her voice sounded harsher than she had intended. Byron threw back the hood.

'I know. The more frivolous I seem, believe me, the more serious I am.' He arched his eyebrows. 'Once we are back in Nottingham, you will prepare your clothes for Robert and I will pay a visit to Sarah, in order to enlist her help...' He was now pacing the room. 'I shall ensure that she is fully aware of her duties, and then the *lendemain* we shall execute our plan.'

He stopped in front of her and placed his hands on her shoulders: 'That is, if you are willing for me to use your house as a safe haven once more?' Lizzie nodded. 'Good, then we are prepared.' Yet he noticed her troubled expression: 'Do not think that I am unafraid,' he said, 'but, hopefully, by this time next week, everything will be different.'

Lizzie met his gaze. His eyes glittered.

'I can arrange for Robert to escape, even to leave the country if necessary,' he said as he sat next to her, 'but what about you? Are you determined to stay in Nottingham? Do you really not want to come with me to London?'

Lizzie hesitated. 'My father may still write to me. He may yet return.'

She felt an unexpected and unwanted knot in her stomach: What if Ben discovered that she was alone once more?

Addressing Byron, she said, 'I know who is really responsible for Mr Betts' death. It was his nephew, Ben Harwood. He told me that now that his uncle was dead, he would inherit everything.' Byron listened intently to her revelation. 'And when I refused to marry him,' she sputtered, 'he tried to force himself on me.'

'But you fought him off?' Lizzie nodded.

'Then we must bring him to justice. But how?'

'Ben used to visit Sarah. He was very keen on her. Perhaps she could trap him somehow?'

'Tomorrow, when we return to Nottingham, I shall propose it to her.'

The coach pulled away from the courtyard and lurched as it ascended the drive. Once on the Nottingham road, the horses picked up speed. Lizzie held onto the seat, the pain in her stomach twisting with every movement of the carriage. Byron noticed that her cheeks were pale. 'You must try not to worry so much. As soon as you are at home, go to bed and wait for me. I shall visit Sarah and return to you immediately. Have courage; I am hopeful of our success.'

He seemed unafraid, even welcoming the challenge. Could she tell him that she may be carrying his child?

Unaware of her thoughts, Byron patted her hand, and laughed.

'What is funny?' Lizzie frowned.

'I'm imagining what your brother will look like in your dress.' He looked into her eyes: 'Perhaps as pretty as you...'

Sarah led her customer up the stairs. 'I wasn't expecting to see you again, Mr Gordon,' she said. 'I thought you were too good to be true; I thought I'd dreamt you.'

'I have returned to haunt you.'

They entered her room and Sarah began to unlace her dress.

'Actually, my dear, I have a different request for you today.'

'I don't blame you if you want it fully clothed; it's so cold at the moment.' She reclined on her bed and drew up her dress, exposing her thighs. Unable to resist the offer, he unbuttoned his breeches and lay over her. She stroked his hair and kissed his cheek. 'That's it, Mr Gordon, you can ask anything you want of me.'

'Well,' he began as he entered her, 'it concerns the fate of Robert Molyneux. He is wrongly imprisoned and I have a plan to rescue him.' Sarah's bed began to creak under their weight.

'How brave,' Sarah gasped. 'How do you mean to do that?'

'I shall wear a disguise and gain entrance to his cell, then he will escape,' Byron panted, 'but, I need someone to distract the guard.' He looked into her eyes: 'Sarah, with your obvious talents, I come to ask you—ah—to perform that task for me.'

Sarah grasped his back: 'Yes, yes, of course I will. I want to see Robert freed as much as you do.'

'There's something else as well,' Byron continued. 'The real culprit must be lured here, and then bound. I shall ensure that the—ah—authorities know where to find him.'

'Who is he? I'd be glad to see him suffer for what he's done to Robert.'

Byron grimaced, 'Ben Harwood.'

Sarah paused: 'Ben? That cheating dog! I'll truss him up like a turkey, don't you worry.' They resumed their energetic rhythm.

'It's not just for me...' Byron drew a sharp breath...'it's as much for Robert's sister, for Lizzie,' he cried out. 'Ah—Lizzie!' He lay motionless for a while on Sarah's breast. A frown spreading over his otherwise satisfied face, he revealed, 'Ben tried to ravish Lizzie.'

'That does not surprise me,' Sarah sighed. She stroked his shoulder. 'I do believe, Mr Gordon, that you care as much for Lizzie as I do for Robert.'

'Then you will help us?' Byron kissed her flushed cheek.

'Definitely! I never thought I would fall in love, but I think I am in love with Robert.' Her eyes were shining in the dim winter light. 'I keep thinking about him. And

dreaming about him... Wishing I could do *this* with him...'
She squeezed Byron's hand. 'Is that what it's like, to be in love?'

Byron nodded. 'Indeed it is.'

'I would like more than anything to be with Robert, somewhere else, far away from Nottingham. I could be faithful to him, I think, given the chance.'

'It is possible, Sarah,' Byron confided, 'that you shall have the opportunity to do just that. Pack all your belongings, and when you leave here tomorrow, it will be for a new life.'

Sarah smiled broadly: 'Will you run away, too? With Lizzie?'

Byron sighed. 'I must go to London no matter what happens. I honestly do not know if Lizzie will accompany me. But I confess that I find myself wanting to be with her, constantly.'

'We're a right pair, aren't we?' Sarah giggled. 'What time do you want me at the prison?'

'Come to the house, *Chez Molyneux*, tomorrow afternoon.'

The pain in Lizzie's stomach was worse, now churning deep within her. How could she tell Byron of her fear? The fear, now almost a certainty, that she was carrying his child. Would he reject her? However would she manage alone with an illegitimate child? Perhaps she could run away with Robert and Sarah, but then, if her father wrote to them, there would be no one to reply. It would be even worse if he returned home to find his children gone. She would have to stay. Would she even survive giving birth? Lizzie tried to push the thought from her mind. She changed from her dress into her nightgown and returned to Byron in the kitchen. She poked the fire, 'Did Sarah agree to the plan?' she asked, hoping her voice sounded calm.

'To every article; and I have had Mr Connor deliver a

letter from Ned Ludd to Colonel Musters, informing him as to the whereabouts of the real murderer.'

A sharp stab of fear shot through Lizzie's stomach. She sat down.

'My dear, are you quite well?' Byron moved nearer to her.

'Yes, I am. I'm just worried about tomorrow.' The pain changed back to a deep ache. She stood. 'I'll make us some tea.'

Byron smiled. 'There is some news which may cheer you. Sarah confessed to me that she is in love with Robert.'

Lizzie turned to him, 'Did she?'

He nodded. 'Poor girl's besotted with him. Says she's even dreaming about him. I could tell that her heart wasn't really in it today. '

Lizzie felt her blood drain from her face. A wave of nausea crept over her. 'Byron—' she began, but was unable to finish the sentence. The room seemed to spin, like an unravelling bobbin. Lizzie felt her knees buckle and her feet slipped from under her.

'When your coach driver informed me as to the address, I confess I was bemused.' Doctor Markham entered the kitchen. Byron closed the door; 'No questions,' he stated.

'Far be it from me to query your lordship's movements. Are you ill, my lord? You seem to me the picture of health.'

'I am. It is not me that has need of a physician.'

Byron showed him into the bedroom. Lizzie lay motionless on her bed. The doctor raised his eyebrows. 'I have to know what happened, in order to make a proper diagnosis.'

'She fainted.'

'Young ladies are prone to it.'

'Not this one. She has never fainted in my company before now.'

The doctor sat next to the bed and took Lizzie's wrist.

'Her pulse is a little fast, but it is strong enough.'

'She's bleeding.' Byron folded his arms.

'Her usual menstruation?'

'How in hell's name would I know?' Byron glared with exasperation.

Doctor Markham lifted Lizzie's nightdress. The bed was soaked in blood.

Byron gasped, 'Christ. Is she dying?'

'I doubt it.' The doctor patted Lizzie's cheek and she opened her eyes. 'My dear,' Markham said, 'I am a doctor. When did you last have a normal bleed?'

'I can't remember,' Lizzie whispered, 'not for months.'

The doctor turned to Byron, 'She appears to be underweight as well. It is a miscarriage—extremely early in the gestation. No more than a couple of months. If the woman's body is not capable of carrying the child to birth, then it will reject it.' He turned to Lizzie, 'We will get you clean, fresh sheets. I would burn these; you'll never get the bloodstains out. And you'll need to keep yourself staunched for a few days, to soak up the blood as you would do normally.'

Lizzie stared at the stranger sitting next to her bed. He patted her hand. 'Do not worry, when you start a family in the future, this should not affect your ability to conceive.'

The doctor stood and returned to the kitchen with Byron. Markham took a small vial from his bag. 'You may administer this: Laudanum, a few drops in warm water every few hours, to ease her pain. Other than that, I suggest you make sure she eats well and that you refrain from sexual intercourse with her. At least until she is stronger,' he sighed. 'And you could take some precautions...' The doctor's stoat-grey eyebrows elevated. 'French letters? I presume you know what I mean.'

Byron nodded. 'Thank you,' he said and shook the doctor's hand.

'This will go no further, I assure you,' said Doctor Markham as he left the house.

Sarah rapped firmly on the door. There was no reply. She knocked again with more fervour. This time she heard the sound of footsteps and the door swung open.

'Must I open the damn door myself?' Ben broke off as he noticed who was standing outside. 'Sarah!' His expression changed and his smile reflected hers: 'I thought you'd become a nun.'

She twirled a lock of her hair, 'Never. I've decided I can't sleep alone for the rest of my life. It wouldn't suit me.' She winked at him.

Ben grinned. 'I thought as much.'

'It's cold out here,' Sarah said, shivering, 'why don't we go to the Angel and we can warm each other up?'

Ben darted back into the hall, snatched up his coat and hurried out of the house, slamming the door behind him. Sarah took his hand and they ran to the inn.

She led him up the stairs and into her room. Immediately he tore off his coat and shirt, unbuttoned his breeches and pulled her onto the bed. Sarah straddled him.

'I know what you want,' she whispered, 'you want me to tie you up, don't you?'

He grinned and raised his hands above his head. She reached over and picked up two stockings then secured both his wrists to the bedposts with firm double knots. She climbed off him.

'What are you doing?' he asked.

'I thought we'd try something a bit different,' she announced, and tied his ankles to the opposite posts at the bottom of the bed.

'Sarah, that's a bit tight,' he frowned.

She put her fingers to her lips and mounted him again. He soon began to moan with pleasure.

'You're being far too noisy,' she gasped, as she reached her climax. 'I've had what I wanted; now you're going to be very, very quiet.'

Before he could object, she took a fifth stocking and pressed it into his mouth. She tied another around his head, gagging him.

'You can still breathe through your nose,' she smirked.

His single cry was muffled and useless; his eyes stared wide open in anger and fear.

'Good, that's too quiet to be heard downstairs.' She climbed off him and straightened her dress. 'Betrayal is quite damnable, isn't it?' she taunted.

She picked up her shawl and loaded the remainder of her few possessions into her bag: her comb, a bottle of lavender oil, and her purse. She reached into Ben's jacket pocket and pulled out all the coins.

'May the Devil dance in your pocket,' she sneered. 'The soldiers will be here soon enough, and then you'll get what's coming to you.' She walked out, slammed the door and locked it behind her.

Ned Ludd's Office, Sherwood.
Monday 13 January 1812
Colonel Musters

If you search upstairs at The Angel tavern in the afternoon of Tuesday 14th January, you will find the murderer of Matthew Betts: his nephew, Benjamin Harwood.

I have it on good authority that the said Mr Harwood bragged about the crime and also to benefitting from the death of his uncle. When dealing with a felony of this nature, one should always ask: 'Cui bono?' that is, 'who stands to gain?' The only person to benefit from Mr Betts' death was Benjamin.

Once more, let me assure you that the framebreaking in which Ben Harwood took part had nothing whatsoever to do with Mr Betts' murder; there was

*never any intention to harm the frameowner. This was
a crime committed alone and totally without my
approval. I trust that you will bring Ben Harwood to
justice with a fitting punishment.*

Ned Ludd

'Drink this, my dear.' Byron helped Lizzie to sit up and
lifted the teacup to her lips. The liquid tasted like bitter
spirit. She coughed.

'What is it?'

'Laudanum. To relieve the pain.'

Lizzie swallowed the diluted alcohol.

'Are you hungry?' Byron stroked her hand.

Lizzie nodded. 'Ravenous,' she murmured.

'So am I. Now that you are awake, I shall go out and
get us something to eat.'

'No, don't leave me,' she whispered. Her hand caught
his sleeve. He sat down once more. 'The doctor has
assured me that you will be well. Lizzie, you are strong.' He
stroked her hair. 'Honestly, you look much better than you
did last night.' In the dying light of the afternoon, his face
reminded Lizzie of a statue in the chapel. Saint Sebastian,
his chest pierced with three arrows, like the heart on the
Three of Swords. A martyr: someone who would rather
die than renounce his beliefs.

'I was so afraid,' Lizzie said.

'So was I.' Byron lifted her hand and kissed it.

'I was afraid that I would die,' Lizzie confessed, 'and I
was afraid that if I lived, you would spurn me, because...'

'Because you were carrying my child?'

Lizzie nodded. Byron kissed the palm of her hand.

'Oh, Lizzie... I am not so much of a rakehell as to cast
you aside for something which you were powerless to
prevent. I was a thousand times more to blame, wasn't I?'

Lizzie shook her head.

'No, I was,' Byron sighed. 'My dear, you may not believe me, but, had you brought a baby Byron into the world, I would have honoured my obligations.'

Lizzie's eyes widened.

'I have already fathered a son...' Byron looked downward: 'I am not proud of the fact, but I have nothing more to do with his mother, and, despite having no guarantee that I am the father, I do send her a regular sum of money. I will not let them suffer.'

Lizzie considered his revelation. He was already a parent and yet providing for his child was reduced to a monthly addition to his bills. The boy may never know his father. How many children had been sired by a seductive man from a privileged family?

'Do you hate me for it?' Byron closed his eyes for a moment. 'I would not blame you.' His steel-blue eyes glinted in the grey gloom.

Lizzie shook her head. 'No, Byron, I do not hate you.' She stroked his cheek. He leant close to kiss her.

'Do you believe in guardian angels?' he asked.

'I don't know,' Lizzie whispered, 'I'm not sure what I believe any more.'

'We should be together.' His expression was impetuous once more. 'Do you think you will be well enough to come to the prison this evening? It has to be tonight, really.'

Lizzie nodded. The pain was now like the familiar dull ache; uncomfortable, but bearable.

'The mail coach leaves at half past seven tonight,' Byron said. 'Robert and Sarah must be on it. My own coach will carry me on to London. I see no reason why you should not accompany me there; live with me as my mistress. The Earl of Berwick means to marry his mistress, and she was a courtesan, an upper-class whore.'

Lizzie opened her mouth to speak, but Byron placed his finger gently against her lips.

'No, do not make the decision now. Let us rescue your brother first, and then we can make our own plans.'

There was a knock at the front door.

'Just a moment,' Byron called. He kissed Lizzie's brow and disappeared into the kitchen.

'I'm ready for our rescue,' Sarah smiled. Byron showed her in.

'There has been a slight change of plan,' he said.

Sarah placed her bag on the kitchen table: 'What's the matter?' She looked around: 'Where's Lizzie?'

'Sarah?' Lizzie called from the bedroom. Sarah hurried in and sat next to the bed.

'Oh, my goodness! What happened to you?'

'You promise not to tell?'

'Cross my heart.' Sarah took her hand.

'I miscarried.'

Sarah looked at Byron who was leaning against the doorway. He nodded and drew a deep breath. 'Yes. It was mine.'

Sarah sighed. 'Don't be afraid, Lizzie. I had the same thing happen to me, last year. Well, not *his*,' she emphasised, 'but a customer's. You will feel better soon.' She smiled at Lizzie and stroked her wrist. 'You need to eat more. You've got bones like a sparrow. I'll get us some food, and then we'll work out how to free Robert.'

'You're wasting your time. There's no one up there.' Emma showed the soldiers up the stairs leading to Sarah's room. The landlady knocked on the door. 'Sarah,' she called, 'Sarah!' She tried the handle.

'Unlock the door, madam.'

Emma lifted a key from her belt and opened the door. She gasped as she surveyed the scene inside. Sarah's clothes and possessions were missing. A naked young man was tied to the bed, barely conscious. In the twilight Emma thought she recognised him.

'Ben?'

'Stand aside.' The captain led his men forward and one of them released Ben's legs. Then he untied his wrists, but left the gag in place. As they dressed him, the captain read from a small piece of paper.

'You are arrested in the name of the King, for the murder of Mr Matthew Betts. You shall be imprisoned until brought to trial at the March assizes.'

They tied Ben's hands behind his back and marched him down the stairs. Emma gazed around Sarah's empty room.

'Where on earth have you gone?' she whispered.

'I am Frère Daniel Corbeille, and I am to hear Monsieur Molyneux's confession.'

The monk's face was concealed by his hood. The guard decided that a friar posed no threat, even if he did sound foreign. He opened the door and let him enter.

'His sister is *avec moi*.'

Lizzie followed Byron inside the prison. The guard showed them to the cell.

'Ten minutes,' he said.

'*Merci*,' Byron said. 'It should not take long.'

Robert dragged himself upright and Lizzie embraced him. 'You are not looking well,' she said.

'Neither are you.' Robert kissed her cheek. 'All day yesterday and last night I had the most fearful stomach ache.'

Byron gazed at the twins: 'It's remarkable,' he murmured in his own voice.

Robert leaned close to him: 'Who are you?' he whispered. 'Are you really here for my confession?'

Byron gave a subtle conspiratorial smile. '*Non, mais je suis votre savieur.*'

Sarah knocked on the prison door. 'I'm here to see Robert Molyneux.'

The guard let her in. 'He's popular today.'

'Oh?' Sarah sounded surprised.

'Got his sister and a priest in there at the moment. He

sounds foreign—French.'

Sarah shook her head. 'Robert has a lot to confess, I should imagine. How long will they be?'

'They're only allowed ten minutes; you'll have to wait.'

Sarah looked disappointed. 'Is that all the time I'll be allowed with him?'

The guard nodded. Sarah gave him a seductive smile. 'I don't suppose you could make a special allowance for me?' She stepped close to him. 'It must be so boring for you standing around here all day and all night. Such lonely work... If I could relieve your burden, might you let me have a few minutes longer?' She placed one hand on the front of his breeches and began to stroke him. She took hold of his hand and placed it inside her bodice so that he could feel her breast.

'Come on,' she whispered. 'Don't tell me that's not fair bargain? No one will know.' She leant back against the wall, unlaced the top of her bodice, and then lifted her skirts.

The guard looked furtively down the corridor. The next watch wasn't due for an hour.

'Why not?' he laughed.

Lizzie peered around the cell door. 'I can't see them,' she whispered.

Byron helped Robert pull Lizzie's spare dress over his head and swiftly laced it. Robert draped her shawl over his head while Byron bundled up the blanket on the bench.

'That ought to do,' he said. He turned to Lizzie: 'You go.'

She darted out of the cell and down the corridor. Turning the corner she caught sight of Sarah, the guard facing her, grunting with increasing volume as he approached a climax. Sarah caught Lizzie's eye as she passed. The guard, buried in his toil, was oblivious to the young woman hurrying down the passage and out of the door.

Lizzie skirted the building and caught her breath. The gabardine sky was pinpricked with a million stars. St Mary's chimed six o'clock. At the bottom of the hill Byron's coach stood waiting. She began to run down the street toward it, but stopped abruptly; she could hear voices, someone approaching from the back of the church. She concealed herself in a doorway and watched as two young soldiers turned up the road toward the gaol, one of them swinging a lantern. If she did not act quickly the plan would be foiled. When they had passed and she was sure they had not seen her, she ran to the church wall and crouched down. She reached into her bag and brought out her pistol. She cocked it and took aim; she held her breath. The bullet shattered the lantern, the oil bursting into flames on the soldier's breeches. He shrieked and attempted to quench the fire, slapping at his leg.

'Get after him, Ned!' he cried. The other soldier ran toward the churchyard. Lizzie had no time to reload her pistol. She scurried silently along the passage next to the railings and watched as the soldier pursued his imaginary assailant down Marygate, his companion limping after him. Lizzie dashed down to the coach. Peter Connor climbed off his seat and opened the door.

'Thought I'd lost you,' he whispered. 'Is his Lordship safe? And the others?'

'They're on their way,' she panted.

'Was that you, setting light to the bloodcoat? Damn good shot.'

'I didn't want to kill him.'

'You did better than that. You put them off the scent, made them go chasing the wild goose.'

Lizzie nodded and climbed inside the carriage. She crossed herself. She prayed that they all would soon be safe, and that Robert would agree to Sarah's plan for them.

'I think that deserves at least twenty minutes,' the guard pulled up his breeches and buttoned them. Sarah smiled at him.

'Thank you,' she whispered, 'I can't tell you how grateful I am.'

At that moment Byron appeared, his arm around Robert dressed in Lizzie's clothes. Robert's face was hidden beneath Lizzie's shawl, pretending to sob.

'The poor child,' Byron opined, 'she is overcome by the *severité* of his crimes.' He turned to Sarah: 'He is almost irredeemable, a lost soul. For the safety of your own soul, my child, come with us, and we shall pray for him.' Byron placed his other arm around Sarah's shoulders. She nodded.

'I will come back tomorrow,' she said to the guard, with tears in her eyes. 'Tell him I shall return.'

Byron addressed the guard: 'All we can do now is pray for a miracle.'

The guard showed the three of them out of the prison. Afterwards he walked down to Robert's cell. In the gloom he could make out the shape of a man lying on the bench.

'Your thrupenny-upright will visit you on the morrow, you lucky dog,' he grunted.

Once inside the coach, Byron removed the monk's robe to reveal his moleskin trousers and silk shirt. Sarah helped Robert remove the dress.

'I don't know who you are, sir, but I will be grateful to you for the rest of my days,' Robert said as he shook Byron's hand.

'Do not thank me, thank Sarah. And thank your sister, for she saved my own skin not long ago.'

Robert's eyes widened. Byron took Sarah's hand and placed it on top of Robert's. 'What this lord has joined together, let no man put asunder.' Robert realised that the coach was moving.

'Where are we going?'

'You and your dear companion are to board the mail coach from the Clinton Arms. There you are to travel to Liverpool. Miss Sarah is eager to become a Mrs, aren't you my dear?'

Sarah nodded. 'Will you sail away with me to the New World, as my husband?'

Robert's eyes shone. 'Of course I will!' He kissed her, clasping her tightly.

'If you can wait that long,' Byron smiled. He turned to Lizzie: 'And you, my dear. Will you not come with me to London? Not even for a short while? I could dress you as a boy; you could pretend to be my page.'

Lizzie's eyes briefly met Robert's. He looked at Sarah, then at Byron. Lizzie shook her head.

'No. I will stay here.'

Robert looked almost as disappointed as Byron. 'Why not?' he asked.

'In case Papa returns. Or if he writes...'

Robert nodded. 'One of us has to be the *responsable*,' he said.

Lizzie sighed, 'I think I have had enough *excitation* to last me a lifetime.'

Byron lifted her hand and kissed it. 'I promise that I will write to you.'

The Nottingham Journal
Saturday 18th January 1812

The Mysterious Case
of the Disappearing Prisoner

On the morning of Wednesday last at the Nottingham Gaol, the guard, making his usual rounds, discovered that the prisoner Robert Molyneux had vanished from his cell. The guard on the night watch said that Mr Molyneux had been visited by a French monk and the prisoner's sister. The guard saw them both leave, along with another young woman who was also intending to visit Mr Molyneux. Her identity and whereabouts are unknown. Miss Lizette Molyneux, the prisoner's sister, when questioned by our journalist, said that Mr Molyneux was definitely in his cell when she visited him. The guard has also sworn under oath that the prisoner was asleep on his bunk when he made the night rounds. Mr Molyneux had been, as it transpired, wrongly imprisoned for the murder of Mr Matthew Betts, Hosier. Mr Betts' nephew, Benjamin Harwood, is now being held awaiting trial for the same murder.

FEBRUARY 1812

Goose feather clouds whirled through the London sky, propelled by the Western wind, teasing the sun with a hint of Spring. Lord Holland embraced his friend on the steps of Whitehall.

'Byron, welcome back to the House. I received your letter.' The two men ascended toward the debating chamber. 'What did you mean about being half a framebreaker yourself?'

He stopped at the top of the steps. Byron turned to him. 'Let us just say that I have a particular interest in the subject. I have a very close connection with the stockingers.'

Holland raised his eyebrows: 'So you will be speaking from the heart, as it were.'

Byron nodded. 'From the heart.'

They entered the building and joined the throng of Lords, milling around on their way to the chamber. One of them looked round and greeted Lord Holland.

'Good day, sir. Damn disgrace this framebreaking business, what? Word has it we're on the brink of a bloody revolution.'

'I do not think it will come to that, Harrowby.' Lord Holland smiled calmly. He gestured to his companion: 'This is Lord Byron. Nottingham is his estate.' The two men bowed. 'The Earl of Harrowby,' Holland introduced, 'Ryder to his friends. Well known for his tolerance and moderation.'

Harrowby laughed, his puffed cheeks latticed with tiny thread-like veins. 'We're not talking tolerance and moderation here...' His expression grew serious. 'Freeing Negroes is one thing, but this is quite another matter. This Bill can't come soon enough in my opinion. The quicker we quell this anarchy the better.' He patted his hands on his bulging belly. The faun-coloured fabric of his embroidered silk waistcoat wrinkled where the buttons were straining to hold it together. 'I hope we can get it over with by lunchtime, I'm starving.'

Byron raised his eyes: 'Are you?' He glared at Harrowby. The Earl was oblivious to Byron's anger.

'I expect you've witnessed these outrages first hand in Nottingham, eh?'

'Yes. I have.'

'If the threat of transportation isn't working, maybe the prospect of the gallows will bring them to their senses,' the Earl sniffed, 'stop them doing it in the first place, what?'

Byron was white with rage. 'I doubt it.'

Lord Holland placed his hand on the young man's shoulder, 'Today you are to make your maiden speech, about this very subject, aren't you, Byron?'

Byron nodded. The Earl of Harrowby blew his nose on a large lace handkerchief. 'Well, good luck with that. I expect I shall encounter you again later on.' With that he was gone.

'That's what you are up against, my friend,' Lord Holland murmured.

Byron and Lord Holland moved along the corridor and entered the chamber. It was even more enormous than

Byron remembered. He admired the vaulted ceiling. Bright shafts of sunlight pierced the room from the leaded windows. They took their seats. Byron gazed around him. He had never spoken in front of such a large audience. Lord Holland remarked on his friend's pallid complexion.

'Byron, you're as white as a sheet,' he whispered. 'Are you quite well?'

Byron rubbed his brow. 'I feel like I might vomit. I believe it is called stage-fright.'

Holland patted him on the back, 'Come now, you're a seasoned actor. Do not fear. There are a great many of us who support you.' Lord Holland leaned closer to him: 'Just imagine you are batting for Harrow, against Eton.' He grinned.

Byron chuckled. 'Thank you. That gives me some confidence. The last time I played cricket against Eton must have been about ten years ago, and we thrashed them.'

'There you are, then.' Holland relaxed on the bench. The Earl of Liverpool rose from his seat, near the woolsack. He called the House to order.

'As the present Frame Bill contains some enactments of a novel nature, it is necessary to state to the House some of the grounds upon which it ought to pass into law. The principal object is to detect offenders. It is deemed necessary to render the offences capital.'

There was a ripple of consternation from Lords on both sides of the House, followed by nods of agreement from others and several men calling, 'Hear, hear!'

'I am aware,' Liverpool continued, 'that there exists more difference of opinion on this than any other point. I, for my part, can see no well-founded objection to try the effects of the measure proposed.' He looked around the chamber, his grey eyebrows furrowed, 'The other House of Parliament are well grounded for sending it up for the concurrence of their Lordships. I now propose that the Bill be read a second time.'

Byron closed his eyes. He thought of Lizzie. The first time he had met her in the street and then her letter asking him for help. How alike Lizzie and Robert were. He felt relieved that Robert and Sarah were now on their way to a new life. But Lizzie, and the other stockingers, were still starving in Nottingham. She had lost his child. His knuckles clenched bone-white. How he wished she had come with him to London. He wished he had abducted her, so that he could return to his rooms triumphant and celebrate by—

'The Noble Lord Byron will now address the House.'

Holland nudged Byron: 'There's your cue,' he whispered.

Byron rose to his feet. He swallowed his fear. He imagined being back at Newstead Abbey, in the Long Gallery, reading his speech to Lizzie on that snowy Sunday.

'...on the day I left the county I was informed that forty frames had been broken the preceding evening, as usual, without resistance and without detection.'

The Earl of Liverpool rolled his eyes. Undeterred, Byron continued, determination and frustration colouring his voice.

'The rejected workmen conceived themselves to be sacrificed to improvements in mechanism. Frames of this description tend materially to aggravate the distress and discomfort of the disappointed sufferers.' Byron met the eyes of the Lords opposite, and he continued, 'But the real cause of these distresses and consequent disturbances lies deeper. When we are told that these men are leagued together not only in the destruction of their own comfort, but of their very means of subsistence, can we forget that it is the bitter policy, the destructive warfare of the last eighteen years, which has destroyed their comfort, your comfort, all men's comfort?'

Byron drew his breath deeply. He tried to relax his shoulders. He ignored the jeers from the benches on the other side of the chamber. 'The government has given aid to Portugal. As their charity began abroad, it should end at home. A much smaller amount would have made the use of the bayonet and the threat of the gibbet unnecessary.'

Lord Holland nodded. Byron gestured his hands forward, palms upward as though presenting a gift. 'But doubtless our friends have too many foreign claims to admit the prospect of domestic relief? I have traversed the seat of war in the Peninsula, I have been in some of the most oppressed provinces of Turkey, but never under the most despotic of infidel governments did I behold such wretchedness in the very heart of a Christian country.'

Byron glared: 'Suppose the law passed. That one of the thousands of stockingers, meagre with famine, sullen with despair, unable to support his family, was dragged into court to be tried for the new offence, by this new law...' He paused for dramatic effect. 'Still,' he said, measuring his words as he neared the end of his speech, 'there are two things wanting in order to convict and condemn him, and these are in my opinion, twelve butchers for a jury and a Jeffreys for a judge!'

His heart was throbbing as he gazed across the chamber. A stunned silence hung for a moment before being broken by cries of 'Hear, hear!' from both sides of the House. He slowly sat down once more. Lord Holland patted him on the back briefly before standing up.

'My Lords. I would first like to compliment my noble friend on his abilities, this being his first speech to the House. I am astonished that the ministers had not thought it proper to reply to it.' He frowned. 'Returning to the Bill, I find it so objectionable that it is my duty to oppose it. I am not surprised at the measure,' a wry smile grew on his lips, 'for I am never surprised at anything foolish coming from the present ministers.' There was a roar of laughter. 'The fact is that such a law has already rendered detection less probable. I have this from the best authority.' He glanced round at Byron.

'Stripped of legal jargon,' Holland waved his hand as if brushing flies away from sugar, 'the Frame Bill amounts to this: Whereas it has been found difficult to detect these offences, we will render that detection more difficult. The absurdity of this is glaring,' Lord Holland glanced at the Earl of Liverpool. 'It is no excuse to say that the law is only temporary. Hanging our fellow subjects is not a proper way of making experiments.'

This time The Lord Chancellor rose to his feet. 'The object is the prevention of the offence. Improvements in machinery are to the advantage of those concerned.' He sat down heavily, as though this was all he had to say on the matter. Byron shook his head. He noticed the Earl of Harrowby nodding on the other side of the chamber. Harrowby stood up, his expression that of a dog that had been disturbed during a nap.

'The offence is, as admitted by everyone, most injurious to the interests of the community. The object of the Bill is to increase detection. The terror of the punishment of death would prevent the commission of the offence.'

Holland jumped to his feet. He held a sheet of paper in front of him. 'I read from the Bill that the threat of capital punishment is not only to be applied for framebreaking, but also for the *intent* to damage machinery or,' he paused, 'breaking a lace thread! I will never consent to put it in the power of the Crown to put a fellow subject to death for damaging a piece of cotton or lace!'

Holland sat down amid cries of agreement. Byron smiled at him and firmly patted his arm. A gentleman with streaks of silver in his temples rose to his feet. 'That's Earl Grey,' Lord Holland murmured to Byron.

'What is the object in proposing this bill? Is it to inflict the death penalty, as my Noble friend Lord Holland has stated? For the *intention* of damaging machinery or fabric?'

Liverpool answered him, 'It is. The mode of carrying that into effect is a matter for discussion in the committee.'

Earl Grey's voice was tinged with exasperation. 'Before

we can vote for a second reading, we ought to be informed as to exactly what offence the Bill is to punish.'

'The intention of government is to inflict the punishment of death instead of transportation; for the originally transportable offences,' Liverpool replied.

An older man stood, his eyes bright and lucid, despite his age. 'This is a strong reason to adjourn the debate.'

'Who is that?' Byron whispered.

Lord Holland squinted. 'Lord Grenville, I believe.'

'Here is a minister,' Grenville continued, 'who has come down to parliament to inflict the punishment of death upon his fellow citizens, but for what offence he does not know!'

Byron snorted. Holland chuckled.

'It is in the ministers' interest that the debate should be adjourned, in order for them to explain what offence they intend to punish with death. I cannot give my consent to the House without knowing this.' Lord Grenville swept his robes back and resumed his seat.

Lord Holland gave an appreciative chuckle as he finished his mouthful of pork chop. He mopped the gravy on his plate with a crust of coarse bread.

'Good idea of yours, coming here, George.' He leant over the table. 'Get away from the Whitehall hurley-burley.'

Byron chewed at his fingernail. 'Even if it does mean mixing with *oi polloi*?' He took up his tankard of ale and gulped. Holland smiled.

'You seem equally at home with both, although your appetite appears to have deserted you.'

Byron had hardly touched his meal. He took up his fork with about as much enthusiasm as a chastened child and attempted to eat a little more potato.

'If you really can't manage it, I'd be glad to finish it for you. That is, if you have no objection.'

Byron placed his cutlery to one side and slid the plate

over to his friend's side of the oak table. Byron did not feel hungry, despite the comforting aroma of ale and gravy.

'I always get a keen appetite after a debate like today,' Holland said, thoughtfully chewing. 'Your speech today was excellent. Worthy of Cicero. You certainly gave them a run for their money, and, ahem, food for thought.'

Byron's eyes were downcast, glinting lead grey in the dim candlelight. 'Didn't do any good, though, did it?'

Holland wiped his mouth with a napkin. He shook his head. 'You can't win every time. That's how government works. On reflection, it is more like tennis than cricket.'

Byron lamented, 'Men don't hang if they lose at tennis.'

Holland rested against the high-backed wooden seat. Byron gazed out the tavern window. There was a silt of ash and grime around the edge. Street traders passed by and the figures of city folk on their way home were distorted by the undulations in the glass.

'When the House divides and the majority vote for a bill, the bill is passed.' Holland finished eating and sipped his beer. He indicated the tankard: 'Superlative ale they keep here, I must say.'

Byron rested his chin on his hand. 'And what if the majority is wrong?'

Holland sighed. 'It really has upset you, hasn't it?' The older man frowned and cocked his head to one side. 'May I give you a word of advice?'

Byron nodded. Holland took out a small snuffbox. He tipped a little into the hollow between his thumb and forefinger then sniffed it up. 'My advice to you, Byron, is to govern your emotions, and not to let them govern you.'

Byron's laugh was hollow..

'At least where politics is concerned,' Holland advised. 'Otherwise you will get yourself in the most fearful pother every time the vote does not go the way you would prefer.'

Byron sighed. He finished his ale. Lord Holland took out his pocket watch.

'Almost four-thirty. I should make my way home.' He

caught Byron's eye, 'It is short notice, but I would like to invite you to an assembly we are having on Monday morning. At Holland House, of course. It may lift your spirits.'

'Thank you,' Byron said. 'I accept.'

'Did you say that you are having a book published next week?'

Byron nodded. '*Childe Harold's Pilgrimage*. It is a poem. I wrote most of it whilst I was abroad.'

Holland hummed approval. 'I look forward to reading it. I have always enjoyed tales of foreign lands. Exotic locations, exotic ladies, eh?' He gave a broad smile. Byron laughed. 'That's better, George,' Holland adjusted his jacket collar. 'You should be proud of yourself. There are not many of us who can lay claim to giving such a memorable speech and publishing their poetry in the space of a few days.'

'I suppose not.' Byron twisted the ring on his finger. Holland stood and shook his hand.

'Rest assured that you did everything you could, when it came to the Frame Bill.'

'Short of challenging the Prime Minister to a duel,' Byron smirked. 'Or at the very least a boxing match.'

Holland exploded with laughter. 'Ha! Now that I would like to see!' He patted Byron's shoulder. 'Until Monday morning. Eleven-thirty.'

MARCH 1812

*J*oan finished stitching the sleeve and broke the thread with her teeth.

'One done,' she said and smiled at Lizzie. 'Thank you for coming to help me.'

'It's no trouble. I enjoy it.'

'The little ones grow so fast. Barely worn their clothes before they've got too big for them.' Joan held up a blue dress dotted with a pattern of flowers. 'This one's Caroline's. I'm going to take it in a little way for Ellie, then I can let it out again when she grows a bit more.'

'Would you like me to do it?'

Joan nodded, 'Please. Only a couple of inches though, either side. Her arms are longer than Caroline's already.' Joan laughed: 'I think she got that from her father.'

Lizzie remembered Byron's arms being too long for Robert's shirt. She felt her cheeks redden. She had tried not to think about Byron, but found that every day something reminded her of him. Lizzie looked at Joan. Her face, although lined was looking less pinched than usual. Lizzie threaded a needle.

'How are the children managing, without their father?'

Joan leaned back in her chair. 'They're bearing up. Michael's finally stopped asking when his Papa's coming back.' She rubbed her eyes. 'I think he now understands what's happened.'

Joan stood and put a kettle on to boil. 'It's not easy on my own. I'm grateful when they're out playing, now that the weather's perking up.' She fetched cups and a teapot. 'Have you heard from Robert?' She spooned black tealeaves from the jar.

Lizzie nodded. 'I had a letter last week.' She drew the letter from her bag. 'I carry it with me everywhere I go. They arrived in New Orleans. Robert says Sarah has a permanent smile. They got married as soon as they arrived. The priest was from one of the Caribbean islands.'

Joan raised her eyes: 'It really is another world, isn't it?' She stirred the tea. 'You'll never tell how he managed to escape from the gaol, will you?'

Lizzie blushed. She shook her head. Joan poured tea for them.

'I don't blame you. Some things are better left unsaid.'

Lizzie finished pinning the dress. She knotted the cotton and began to make neat stitches.

'Hold your frigging horses!' Emma shouted to whoever was hammering on the door of The Angel. She unbolted it and slid back the lock. 'I'm not open yet. If you've brought the second barrel from the brewers, you're going to have to come back later for the payment—' She broke off as she realised that the boy standing outside was not rolling a barrel, but carrying a large parcel wrapped in thick paper. A red ribbon was tied around the package. 'What on earth?' Emma looked askance. 'Are you playing a paw-paw trick, lad?'

'I've brought it off the mail coach.' The youth was dressed in dark travelling clothes, his boots spattered with mud. 'It's for a Miss Lizette Moly-Molly-Molyneux.

Addressed to The Angel tavern. It's been sent from London.'

Emma raised her eyes.

'Are you Miss Molyneux?'

Emma laughed. 'No, lad, I'm not. But I'll see that she gets it. Emma fetched a coin from behind the bar. 'For your trouble delivering it.' The boy bit the coin to check its authenticity. 'Do you take me for a prigger?' Emma snorted.

'No, Madam, but when you've seen as many tawdry tanners as I have, you can't be too careful.'

Emma smiled. 'Off with you!' The lad trotted away toward town.

'For me?' Lizzie let Emma into her kitchen. Emma slid the package onto the table. 'It's heavy, feels like a Bible.'

Lizzie frowned. 'From London?'

Emma nodded. Lizzie untied the red silk ribbon and began to remove the packaging. A small piece of folded paper lay on top of a large book. Instantly she recognised the handwriting on the paper: *For my dearest Lizzie*. She sat down. 'I know whom it is from,' she murmured.

Emma smiled. 'Thank goodness. I wasn't going to lug it back again.' Lizzie was silent. 'I have to get back to The Angel. I'm expecting a barrel to be delivered this morning.' She glanced at the book: 'It'd take me forever to read that! I hope it's worth it.'

'It will be,' said Lizzie. 'It was...'

Emma let herself out of the door. Lizzie lifted up the letter. She closed her eyes and imagined him writing it. She laid it to one side, wanting to prolong the enjoyment. She opened the cover of the book, the title embossed on the surface in gold letters. The edges of the pages looked as though they had been brushed with silver. On the first page, under the title and the name of the author, there was a line of handwriting: *To my dearest Lizzie, With fondest memories, B*

'My sweet lord,' she whispered. She took a knife and slit the seal on the folded paper.

8, St James' Street, London
Sunday 15th March 1812

My Dearest Lizzie,

When you hear about what has been happening to me lately, you will forgive my silence.

I hope that you will find the enclosed parcel pleasing— you may recognise some of the traits of Harold as my own, however as you know me, then you will also discern that we are quite different in temperament.

Now I am enjoying being a lion *in London. As you predicted, I am receiving adoration and adulation! There are a great many young ladies here who make it their goal to* ensnare *me, and on the most part fail to do so for any length of time, as they are insincere and, I believe, are in love with a phantom rather than the real man.*

As you suggested to me, I have resolved to meet with my sister, Augusta, again. Her affection and her amusing conversation will be a welcome distraction from the giddiness of assemblies, parties and dinners which, as a famous author, I feel obliged to attend.

I expect you have heard, or read, that my speech, although well received, did not prevent the passing of the Frame Bill. At least Robert has his liberté *and* fraternity—*it was too much to hope for* egalité *in this country.*

Heigh-ho. Sometimes I long for the peace of Newstead. I shall never forget our time together in Nottingham, especially at Newstead, and I shall not forget you. If you ever need my aid, you may write to me at the above address, where I will be for the foreseeable, being a captive animal in the Capital. Otherwise, say the word and I will send you a letter of introduction to one of the dressmakers in London to secure your employment.

Now my dear girl, I shall retire to bed as it is after three o'clock in the morning and I must rest before facing my fanatical audience tomorrow. I am due at Holland House again at seven in the evening—so I shall have to rise by two p.m. in order to be dressed properly for the occasion! I expect you will find this très amusant, *having dressed and undressed me yourself.*

I wish you all the bonne chance *in the world. You were a lamp in my* obscurité *and lit up my heart with your dark enlightenment.*

I   remain   with   all amour—propre *(and* impropre*),*
most affectionately,
your Captain Ludd,
Byron

1812 – 2012
REFLECTION
AND REVOLT

'We are the 99% they are the 1%'

*B*ritain was in the grip of recession. The government had spent a fortune on foreign wars. People in positions of power had gambled away huge sums and the public were squeezed to bail them out. 1811 and 2011 had many similarities. Starvation is not currently the fate of those left in poverty in this country, but malnutrition is. Mass unemployment, failing banks and laughably low interest rates have made the public lose any trust they had in authority. As I write, the protesters in Syria are attacked by the military. All around the world the 'Occupy' movement has resurrected the spirit of Ned Ludd: the ordinary people have had enough of greedy capitalism gambling with their lives, taken to the streets and made their voices heard. The (former) Archbishop of Canterbury has leant his support to the movement, saying that the true spirit of Christianity has more to do with ordinary people, kindness, charity and compassion than it has to do with 'the Tory party at prayer.'

2012 marks the 200th anniversary of Lord Byron's maiden speech to the House of Lords. What would he have made of Britain in the twenty-first century? An uneasy Coalition government beset by in-fighting and indecision would have no doubt given him prime material for satire. Would he have exhorted the British people to look to Greece for inspiration? Revolt against so-called 'austerity' measures which seem engineered to hit the poorest and most vulnerable people the hardest. Our Prime Minister praises the Egyptian people and others who have overthrown oppressive leaders in the 'Arab Spring' but condemns British citizens who want to do the same here. He condemns the oppressive regimes and inequality in those countries, but is hell-bent on implementing similar policies here. The gap between the 'haves' and the 'have nots' is growing into a similar gulf that existed in the Regency period. When there is a sizeable majority with lower living standards and expectations than the minority in power, then the possibility of revolution increases. Those with nothing left to lose, they are truly dangerous.

©Christy Fearn, Nottingham January 2012

Made in the USA
Charleston, SC
17 May 2013